JAKOB VON GUNTEN

Jakob von Gunten

a novel by Robert Walser 1878 - 1956

Translated and with an Introduction
by Christopher Middleton

UNIVERSITY OF TEXAS PRESS
AUSTIN AND LONDON

Standard Book Number 292–70015–6
Library of Congress Catalog Card Number 75–108962
Copyright © 1969 by Helmut Kossodo Verlag
All rights reserved
Printed by The University of Texas Printing Division, Austin
Bound by Universal Bookbindery, Inc., San Antonio

INTRODUCTION

Jakob von Gunten is one of several narratives of its period which transformed the world of German fiction. It is unlike any other German novel, and unlike any other work of European fiction. First, though, one has to realize that the German novel had for a long time been a compendium of writing in all shapes and sizes. So the journal form of *Jakob von Gunten*, subtitled "Ein Tagebuch," was not something freakish. At the time when it was written (1908), the crux was a refining of the novel's customary gross form into more compact and elementary forms. Whereas in older novels soliloquy (with introspection) had been one element among others, this element was now becoming independent. More, it was becoming analytic. So one might call *Jakob von Gunten* an analytic fictional soliloquy. That sounds, true enough, very portentous. In reality, the book is more like a capriccio for harp, flute, trombone, and drums.

Three other fictions of the time show what mode of experience was shaping the transformation of the novel: Musil's *Törless* (1906), Carl Einstein's *Bebuquin* (1909), and Rilke's *The Notebooks of Malte Laurids Brigge* (1910). In each book, the hero explores remote and perilous regions of his mind; with perceptions of snailhorn delicacy he maps a shifting "inner world" of feelings and impulses; and he pursues a primal enigmatic reality dwelling somehow between the perilous inner world and the brutish disorder of the external world. Strindberg in Paris had started it with his *Inferno* (1896). In 1910 Kafka, soon to become master of the absurd, was starting to write his journal, and was already familiar with Walser's prose, which he liked. During these four years, 1906–1910, the point of leverage for a revolution in German fiction was being determined. The spirit, at all events, was crystalizing in the disparate imaginations of these writers: Rilke in Paris; in Berlin—unknown to one another—Musil, Einstein, and Walser; and Kafka in Prague. These cities form a neat right angle across the heart of Europe. Still on the fringe, by Lake Constance, lived another writer who was later to evolve his own form of soliloquy (and who also admired Walser) : Hermann Hesse.

Yet one fails to define Walser by placing him like this among certain crucial "historical developments." Little known as he still is, he was one of the liveliest writers of his time; also he was a sophisticated writer. But his language is peculiar, because it is so unliterary (or what name should be given to this kind of intensity? When a new mode of imagining erupts into literature, it dislocates the rhetoric of its time, and is of subtler stuff than that rhetoric—"the infinite arrives barefoot on this earth," says Hans Arp). It would be silly to regard Walser as an intellectual writer in the way that, say, Hofmannsthal, Thomas Mann, or Kafka were intellectual writers. Once, in Berlin, he actually said to Hofmannsthal at a party: "Couldn't you forget for a bit that you're famous?" No, Walser's writing does retain, to the end of his anguished years as a writer, an eccentricity as balanced and as clownishly serious as the paintings of Henri Rousseau. In the framework of the developments sketched above, he stands apart. He is, in significant ways, untutored: something of a "primitive." His prose can display the essential luminous naiveté of an artist who creates as if self-reflection were not a barred door but a bridge of light to the real. It is no coincidence that his twenty-five years of writing cover almost exactly the period when "naive" art was being discovered in the West: as a marvel of technique, as a revelation of wonder ranging from the most exotic dreams to the most banal things (while freely swapping their appearances)—new and joyous metaphors for a doddering civilization, and energy for Hamlet's heirs.

Walser was born in Biel, Central Switzerland, in 1878. His father, Adolf, owned a small bookbindery with stationery and toy shop attached. His mother, Elisa Marti, came from a family of country nailsmiths in Schangnau. Not far off in the background was the less lowly paternal grandfather, Johann Ulrich Walser (1798–1866), until 1837 an outspoken liberal-utopian pastor, who became a journalist and founded his own newspaper, *Das Basellandschaftliche Volksblatt*. Adolf and Elisa had eight children: four boys, a girl, two more boys, then another girl. Three of the boys were to distinguish themselves: the second, Hermann (1870–1916) became a professor of geography at Bern University, and Karl (1877–1942) became one of the outstanding stage-designers and book-illustrators of the time (he is the model for the brother described by Jakob von Gunten). Lisa (1874–1944) was also a remarkable person. She ran the household when the mother became mentally deranged, then, with some financial help from an uncle (Friedrich Walser, an architect in Basel), she studied at a seminary in Bern and became a teacher. It was to this strange and beautiful spinster that Walser often looked for guidance during his nomadic life.

He left school when he was fourteen, and worked for a while as a clerk in a bank. Then in 1895 he went to Stuttgart, to work in a publishing house (though he hoped to become an actor). He came to Zürich in the autumn of 1896. In Zürich and several other eastern Swiss towns he earned a living with various odd jobs for the next nine years. His first poems appeared in the Bern newspaper *Der Bund* in May 1898. Soon after this, he met the elegant *littérateur* Franz Blei in Zürich, who described him as follows: "A tall, rather gawky lad, with a bony reddish-brown face, over which stood an uncombable shock of fair hair,[1] greyish blue dreamy eyes, and beautifully shaped large hands which came out of a jacket with sleeves too short and didn't know where to go and would have liked best to be stuck into his trouser pockets so as not to be there." During this period, Walser was writing his first prose pieces, in which the clerk (*commis*) appears as a special kind of underdog. The *commis* as underdog was a figure who greatly interested the young Kafka in Prague. The period entailed a visit (or two) to Munich (1899? and 1901): the writers associated with the new magazine *Die Insel*—Otto Julius Bierbaum, Alfred Walter Heymel, and Rudolf Alexander Schröder—were curious about his work and published poems of his, some prose, and some miniature plays in verse. Walser's first book, *Fritz Kochers Aufsätze*, was published by Insel Verlag in 1904, with illustrations by Karl. It was during the previous year, 1903, that Walser had worked as assistant to an unsuccessful inventor, Karl Dubler-Grässle, at Wädenswil near Zürich: this supplied the setting for his second novel, *Der Gehülfe* (1908). His first novel, *Geschwister Tanner* (1906), is a meandering impressionist version of his wanderings in East Switzerland, and concerns his relations with Lisa and Karl.

In the spring of 1905, Walser went to live in Berlin. Here he stayed at first with Karl, in Charlottenburg. Karl was by now making his name as an illustrator, and working also as a stage designer for Max Reinhardt. Fraternal relations were sometimes

---

[1] Later documents attest to a darker russet color (so does a photograph of Walser in Berlin, complete with wing collar and mustache).

very close, sometimes strained. Both were tall strong men, peculiar men, whose jokes at genteel Berlin parties could often seem excessively bucolic. Expelled and thrust into a cab, they would exit through the far door and grinningly confront their exasperated host, over and again, as he stood there each time dusting his hands. When Karl was away, Robert had the apartment to himself, except for Karl's cat. During one such spell he wrote *Geschwister Tanner*, in six weeks, on a diet of sprats (shared presumably with the cat). Christian Morgenstern read the manuscript for the publisher Bruno Cassirer, and recommended it—Walser, he wrote, "sees the world as a perpetual miracle" (but he told Walser by letter that the writing was errant). It was before this that Walser, soon after his arrival in Berlin, attended a school for servants and then worked, during the winter of 1905, as butler—Monsieur Robert—in a Silesian château (Schloss Dambrau). In the later story, "Tobold," he described how nice it was to tread across the Persian rugs at nightfall, carrying freshly lit lamps into quiet rooms. The school for servants was to become material for the Benjamenta Institute of *Jakob von Gunten*. The role of servant accorded with Walser's passion for the minimal: elementary happenings and small private feelings which he calls "the true truths." Max Brod, one of his first admirers, appositely remarked: "After Nietzsche, Walser had to come." Or, as Walser himself said: "God is the opposite of Rodin."

During his Berlin years, 1905–1913, Walser was writing steadily at his shorter prose pieces, many of them *feuilletons* for literary magazines. His living remained precarious. Bruno Cassirer helped him financially until about 1908, and even offered him the chance of a trip to India. Walter Rathenau, likewise, offered to find him a job on Samoa; and the publisher Semmy Fischer asked him to travel in Poland and Turkey. All such invitations were refused. In *Geschwister Tanner*, Simon says: "I'm staying here. It's nice, just to stay. Does nature go abroad? Do trees travel, to acquire greener leaves elsewhere and then to come back and show themselves off?" The shorter prose pieces were collected in the books *Aufsätze* (1913), *Geschichten* (1914), and *Kleine Dichtungen* (1914), all published by Kurt Wolff, who was then a leading avant-garde publisher. It is also said that Walser wrote three other novels during this time, all of them lost. The end of the Berlin period came with increasing poverty. The story "Frau Wilke" (in *The Walk and Other Stories*, London, 1957) can be read as an evocation of life in one of his last lodgings in a Berlin suburb (Schöneberg?): a ruinous room, imagined wistfully to have been once, perhaps, the lodging of a baron, or of an earl. The publication in 1909 of his poems (*Gedichte*) and of *Jakob von Gunten* seems not to have made any appreciable change in his material existence. Nor does his period of work as secretary in the Neue Sezession art gallery. It was probably in the middle of the Berlin period that he traveled by balloon from Bitterfeld to the Baltic coast, in company with Paul Cassirer (director of the Neue Sezession) and a good stock of cold cutlets and liquor. The up-and-coming Expressionists of the time (also those being published by Kurt Wolff) seem not to have known of him—Jakob van Hoddis, Georg Heym, Franz Pfemfert, Kurt Hiller, Franz Werfel, Herwarth Walden, Johannes Becher, none mentions him.[2] With Alfred Lichtenstein he might have got on happily. Lichtenstein's prose has a bedevilled clownish irony with strong affinities to Walser.

In the spring of 1913, Walser left Berlin and traveled back to Switzerland. He spent the next seven years in and around Biel. To

[2] It is just possible that Jakob van Hoddis is referring to Walser (perhaps quoting him) in his "Über die deutsche Sprache," published in *Die Aktion* in 1914 (Volume 4, No. 9, p. 187). He wrote: "Wie liebe ich den armseligen Dichtersmann, der die Sätze schreibt: 'Und jener Ballsaal erstrahlte in einer tobenden, gedankenübertäubenden Nachdenklichkeit.' "

start with, he lived in one of the three rooms of his sister Lisa's apartment. He saw hardly anyone except her and her friend Frieda Mermet, who soon became a good friend to Walser. During this time he published four books of prose pieces, including the longer work *Der Spaziergang* (1917), and in 1919 his four miniature plays, *Komödie*. By now it was hard for him to find a German publisher, not least because of the war. For most of the time he lived in the attic of the Hotel zum blauen Kreuz. A visitor (Ernst Hubacher) described his room as follows: "There was only a bed, a table, and a chair. A cheap map of Europe was tacked to the wall." Walser worked, clad in a military greatcoat and slippers which he had made from old bits of clothing.

Then in 1920 he took a job as an archivist in Bern; after six months of it, he left the job, but he stayed in Bern. He was working on a novel, *Theodor*, which has not survived (another novel of the Biel period, *Tobold*, was also lost, or destroyed). The prose of the Bern period (1920–1929) is a very complicated matter. We have the book *Die Rose*, published by Rowohlt in Berlin in 1925. But there are also masses of other short prose pieces which appeared in magazines and newspapers in Zürich, Berlin, and Prague. There are important stylistic and thematic changes during this period. The stylistic invention ranges between maximum abruptness and beautifully timed arabesque dottiness. There is also an abstruse conflict going on in this prose between the spontaneous "primitive" Walser and the ironic self-reflective Walser of nightmare and psychic distress. Painstaking editorial work by Jochen Greven has solved many of the problems (*Festzug*, volume VII of the *Gesamtwerk*, 1966). The problems involved deciphering and dating about eight hundred prose pieces and dialogues in a microscopic script. This script was not a cipher system, as some scholars had supposed, but a kind of personal shorthand. Jochen Greven has established that some three hundred of these curious texts are versions of pieces extant in print or normal script, while some five hundred are either not identifiable or not decipherable. Greven has emphasized that the script was not a symptom of psychosis, but was habitual to Walser for drafting his work and had been so since the Biel years.

Walser's remaining productive years, while he was living in Bern, were a time of acute trouble for him. He corresponded with a few friends, like Frieda Mermet and Resy Breitbach. He kept changing his lodgings. He took long walks, as ever. He kept writing. It is a story with many dark corridors: the people in the streets of Bern saying audibly as he passed by, "That fellow belongs in the madhouse"; Walser stubbornly resisting a few attempts by the paltry Swiss literary establishment to net him; the continued apathy of the reading public, despite loyal acceptance by such editors as Max Rychner in Zürich and Otto Pick in Prague. Walser was alone; he was without means; once or twice he attempted suicide. Eventually, early in 1929, Lisa persuaded him to enter the Waldau psychiatric clinic, which he did, voluntarily. In 1933 he moved to the asylum at Herisau in Canton Appenzell—still quiet in his ways. In July 1936 he was visited by Carl Seelig, the Swiss writer. For many years they used to take walks together, and in 1944, after Lisa's death, Seelig became Walser's legal guardian and financial support. Their conversations are to be found in Seelig's book *Wanderungen mit Robert Walser* (1957). Walser conscientiously wrote no more ("I'm not here to write, but to be mad"). Yet he could display an astonishing memory of other men's writings, French, German, Russian, and English. Certain remarks also show that he recognized, not without bitterness, his fate as an artist of the infinitesimal, eclipsed by grander scribes—the "imperialists," like Thomas Mann, as he said. He died on Christmas Day in 1956, while out for a walk on his own.

I have drawn a profile of Walser as an elusive deviant in a pattern of changes affecting the world picture of German fiction. Not losing sight of this deviancy, I want now briefly to note some ways in which *Jakob von Gunten* relates to some factors in tradition and to certain signs of its time. Some readers may want to ignore these notes and others may find them helpful once they have read the book. I offer these remarks as notes and suggestions only: the last thing I want to do is "fix" a perspective in literary-historical terms.

(1) Jakob's journal is a record, *impromptu*, of moment-to-moment life in the Benjamenta Institute. He is a boy, seventeen years old perhaps, who has run away from home in a remote province. The framework of improvisation, which suited Walser's temperament, contains Jakob's life design. This design assumes the form of successive small waves of time, etching on Jakob's sensibility their contours and contents. Constant in the flux, as fact and fantasy collude, is Jakob's passion for surprise, for paradox, and for self-knowledge. There are all kinds of ribbings and ripplings across the surface of Jakob's record. After Lisa Benjamenta's death, Kraus solemnly says: "When we eat, the fork will tell us how thou hast desired us to handle and manage it, and we shall sit decently at table, and the knowledge that we are doing so will make us think of thee." This oddness is straight. Then one asks: or is it? One should not identify Jakob and Walser. They have much in common, but the book is not a self-portrait.

(2) The Benjamenta Institute. It certainly makes fun of fictions like Goethe's 'Turmgesellschaft' (in *Wilhelm Meisters Wanderjahre*); does it matter whether the fun is deliberate or not? Other such reformatory groupings in Germany around the turn of the century were the George Circle, and the Charon Circle, the 'Goethebund,' the 'Dürerbund,' the Darmstadt 'Künstlerkolonie,' Johann Müller's 'Freistatt persönlichen Lebens,' and the 'Wandervögel.' Thirty-five years before *Jakob von Gunten*, Nietzsche

had seen Bayreuth as a center of cultural regeneration (before it became sanctimonious); thirty-five years after *Jakob von Gunten*, there is Hesse's Kastalien (*Das Glasperlenspiel*). The German dream of integrating the individual and of an élite to spearhead cultural and social reform—Walser's book was a new variant on this, if not a parody of it. The pretensions of maturity, and the intellectual pride, are tacitly annihilated, without brutish anti-intellectualism, for once. Jakob says: "I value the way in which I open a door. . . . The generations of men are losing the joy of life with all their treatises and understandings and knowledge. . . . I like running down stairs. What a lot of talk!"

Yet the idea of decadence (*Entartung*) is a real presence in the book. The bourgeois runaway Jakob wants to become a zero, to start from all the way down. It is the process which Sartre was later to call the "withdrawal of the projections." Walser's clown-ishness, and Jakob's boyish critique of "cultivated circles," do occupy an eccentric position in a great and fateful dynamic of ideas. Nietzsche, in *Zarathustra*, had presented the child as an imago of free creative life, of Dionysian folly free from violation by intellect. Naive and primitive art figure pre-eminently in Kandinsky's and Marc's *Der blaue Reiter*, 1912. Morgenstern called the child in man the "deathless creator" in him. By 1916, Hugo Ball was calling his fellow Dadas the "infants of a new age." The birth of a "new man" was the first concern in Expressionist drama of the time. In 1919, Louis Aragon published his infantile novel *Quelle âme divine* (*Littérature*, October 1919). Three other artists who cultivated "childishness": Paul Klee, George Grosz, Kurt Schwitters.

(3) The *déclassé* bourgeois Jakob: Kraus, the real proletarian, is aggressively suspicious of him to the end. The future is here foreshadowed: all those middle-class European intellectuals and

writers who stood desperately with the proletariat when the wave of revolution struck: Dada in Berlin, Johannes Becher, Ernst Toller, Bert Brecht, Franz Jung—everywhere a wish for new life coming "from the lower depths."

(4) *Mysterium*. On his arrival, Jakob thinks that there is a mystery at the heart of the Institute. He imagines a castle, with palatial rooms, dancing, even an Englishman, somewhere behind the scenes. Possibly this fantasy of a castle attracted Kafka when he read the book. Even more so, the fact that it is a Castle of Disenchantment. Once Jakob has penetrated to the hidden areas, he finds just a goldfish tank which he and Kraus have to keep clean. Yet an initiation does take place before this; and there is a mystery being enacted, if not in physical space, then in Jakob's mental space. Lisa Benjamenta, as psychogogue, leads Jakob down into a subterranean region, interior of the earth-womb, for a rebirth. The ceremony even starts like a Greek Orphic initiation ("Look, Jakob, there will be darkness all around you"). We hardly know if it is "for real" or if Jakob is having one of his fantasies while he waits for his supper.

For all his blithe chirping, Jakob is an ambiguous creature: "Together with you, one can venture either something courageous or something very delicate," says Herr Benjamenta. Essences of Rimbaud, Holden Caulfield, and Walter Mitty flit in and out of him. A curious fate for religion here: when Fräulein Benjamenta dies, there is ritual, but no religion. She has said: "Singing is praying." A simple "faith" does not prevent Jakob from ignoring God or keeping him out of reach—"there are no gods, only one, and he's too sublime to help."

5) Jakob is also pedantic, didactic, sententious, and a bit of a snob. And so was Charlie Chaplin. (The didacticism in Walser is much milder and more ironic than in many Swiss writers. Its

basis in feeling is volatile: "Heartfelt emotions put something like an icy coldness into my soul. If there's immediate cause for sadness, the feeling of sadness entirely escapes me.")

(6) The language. Two features are precocious vocabulary and eccentric syntax. Jakob airily says: "Sometimes I say things that surpass by own understanding." His use of (Walserian) abstract words is not just improbable, it is also, at times, inept (once or twice he has to check himself). Kraus's vocabulary is, on occasion, also set askew to his outline as a character. These are positive factors. It is the delicate art of ineptitude, which Walser kept alive in an age of gloomy professional polish and literal-minded expertise. Creation entails distortion, and Walser's distortions are timed and shaped with tact (like vivid free forms in non-representational art). Even then, Jakob's talk is often enough Walser's talk: that of an unsleeping accurate dreamer who had only irony for the somnolent cerebralizings of his day.

There is play with the notion of breathless story-telling. When a terrified Jakob rushes up with something urgent to say, he goes off into an elaborate Homeric simile about Goliath, with all kinds of embroidering, before getting to the point. A mischievous blocking of "dramatic thrust," also a parody of "epic breadth." There is also a type of sentence that starts, halts, turns a corner, almost dances backwards, then, quite suddenly, has arrived: "Kraus, it was he, rushed breathless and pale, and unable to deliver the message which he had, obviously, on his lips, into the room" (the translation follows the original). This can be done for the sake of the dance; but the example given is thoroughly functional. Generally, Walser's language is a dance rather than a walk. One should notice, too, the small dialogic nuances in Jakob's monologues: small linking phrases that vibrate with tacit questions or answers. This corrugates the surfaces: planes shift to reveal supporting volumes.

Some dialogues can be as wooden as Jakob's occasional old-fashioned pose as a writer: "It's time I laid down my pen." There are also the moments, like the visits to Johann's apartment, where the prose lands among mandarin platitudes. One is reminded of the dialogue in Henri Rousseau's play *La vengeance d'une orphéline russe*.

The fiction of the journal is sustained, even though it becomes improbable here and there—the last few sections, for example, which seem more like straight narrative. One need not question such points too closely: Walser's art is impulsive, even aleatory (his special genius in the short prose piece shows this).

(7) Jakob's last dream. Epiphany of Don Quixote and Sancho Panza, as Benjamenta and Jakob ride into the desert, refugees from culture. The picaresque form is interiorized in *Jakob von Gunten*. The old episodic series of actions, as in *Don Quixote*, becomes an episodic series of reflections and fantasies. Ghostly presence here of one of the oldest forms of European fiction. The Quixote-Panza epiphany is no random matter.

Christopher Middleton

BIBLIOGRAPHY

Books in German

Robert Walser, *Dichtungen in Prosa* (edited by Carl Seelig), volumes I–V, 1953, f. Geneva and Hamburg, Verlag Helmut Kossodo. This edition will include a further five volumes edited by Jochen Greven: *Das Gesamtwerk*. Volumes VI–VII appeared in 1966.

Robert Walser, *Jakob von Gunten: ein Tagebuch*. Berlin: Bruno Cassirer, 1909. New edition, Zürich: Steinberg Verlag, 1950. Other translations: into French, by Marthe Robert, 1960; into Serbo-Croat, by Slavko Grbesic, 1963.

Robert Mächler, *Das Leben Robert Walsers*. Geneva and Hamburg: Verlag Helmut Kossodo, 1966.

Other translations

Christopher Middleton: Robert Walser, *The Walk and Other Stories*. London: John Calder, 1957. Also 'A Village Tale' in *Great German Short Stories* (edited by Stephen Spender), New York: Dell, 1960; 'Masters and Workers,' 'Pierrot,' 'Helbling's Story' in *Texas Quarterly*, Vol. VII, No. 3 (Autumn, 1964).

Harriett Watts: 'The Little Berliner' in *Delos*, 1, 1968.

Michael Bullock: *The Assistant* (*Der Gehülfe*). London: Calder & Boyars, 1969.

Some articles

J. C. Middleton, "The Picture of Nobody: Some Remarks on Robert Walser, with a note on Walser and Kafka." *Revue de langues vivantes,* 24, 1958.

George Avery, "A Poet beyond the Pale." *Modern Languages Quarterly,* 24, 1963.

Christoph Siegrist, "Robert Walsers kleine Prosadichtungen." *Germanisch-Romanische Monatsschrift,* 17, 1967.

Articles by Jochen Greven, Martin Walser, and others, in the special issue of the periodical *Text + Kritik,* 12, edited by Wolf Wondratscheck: Göttingen, 1966.

JAKOB VON GUNTEN

One learns very little here, there is a shortage of teachers, and none of us boys of the Benjamenta Institute will come to anything, that is to say, we shall all be something very small and subordinate later in life. The instruction that we enjoy consists mainly in impressing patience and obedience upon ourselves, two qualities that promise little success, or none at all. Inward successes, yes. But what does one get from such as these? Do inward acquisitions give one food to eat? I would like to be rich, to ride in coaches and squander money. I have discussed this with Kraus, my school-friend, but he only shrugged his shoulders in scorn and did not honor me with a single word of reply. Kraus has principles, he sits firmly in the saddle, he rides satisfaction, and that is a horse which people should not mount if they want to do some galloping. Since I have been at the Benjamenta Institute I have already contrived to become a mystery to myself. Even I have been infected by a quite remarkable feeling of satisfaction, which I never knew before. I obey tolerably well, not so well as Kraus, who has a masterly understanding of how to rush forward helterskelter for commands to obey. In one thing we pupils are all similar, Kraus, Schacht, Schilinski, Fuchs,

Beanpole Peter, and me, all of us—and that is in our complete poverty and dependence. We are small, small all the way down the scale to utter worthlessness. If anyone owns a single mark in pocket money, he is regarded as a privileged prince. If anyone smokes cigarettes, as I do, he arouses concern about the wastefulness in which he is indulging. We wear uniforms. Now, the wearing of uniforms simultaneously humiliates and exalts us. We look like unfree people, and that is possibly a disgrace, but we also look nice in our uniforms, and that sets us apart from the deep disgrace of those people who walk around in their very own clothes but in torn and dirty ones. To me, for instance, wearing a uniform is very pleasant because I never did know, before, what clothes to put on. But in this, too, I am a mystery to myself for the time being. Perhaps there is a very very commonplace person inside me. But perhaps I have aristocratic blood in my veins. I don't know. But one thing I do know for certain: in later life I shall be a charming, utterly spherical zero. As an old man I shall have to serve young and confident and badly educated ruffians, or I shall be a beggar, or I shall perish.

We pupils, or cadets, have really very little to do, we are given hardly any assignments. We learn the rules by heart. Or we read in the book *What Is the Aim of Benjamenta's Boys' School?* Kraus is also studying French, on his own, for there are no foreign languages or suchlike things on our timetable. There is only a single class, and that is always repeated: "How Should a Boy Behave?" Basically, all our instruction is centered on this question. We are not taught anything. There is a shortage, as I said before, of teachers, that is to say, the educators and teachers are asleep, or they are dead, or seemingly dead, or they are fossilized, no matter, in any case we get nothing from them. Instead of the teachers, who for some strange reason really are lying around like dead men, and sleeping, a young lady instructs and rules us, Fräulein Lisa Benjamenta, the sister of the Principal. She comes, with a small white cane in her hand, into the classroom and the class. We all stand up at our desks when she appears. Once she has sat down, we are allowed to sit down also. She gives three sharp and imperious knocks on the edge of her desk, and the instruction begins. What instruction! But I would be telling lies if I found it curious. No. I find the things that Fräulein Benjamenta teaches us adorable. It is little, and we are always revising, but perhaps there is some mystery hidden behind all these nothings and laughable things. Laughable? We boys of the Benjamenta Institute never feel like laughing. Our faces and our manners are very serious. Even Schilinski, who is still a complete child, laughs very seldom. Kraus never laughs, or, when he is carried away, he gives a very short laugh only, and then he is angry that he let himself be drawn into adopting such a prohibited tone. Generally, we pupils do not like to laugh, that is to say, we are hardly able to any more. We lack the requisite jolliness and airiness. Am I wrong? God knows, sometimes my whole stay here seems like an incomprehensible dream.

The youngest and smallest of us pupils is Heinrich. One can't help feeling gentle toward this young man, without thinking anything of it. He stands quietly in front of shopwindows, quite absorbed by the sight of the goods and of the tasty things in there. Then he usually goes in and buys some sweets for six groschen. Heinrich is still a complete child, but he already talks and behaves like a grown person, with good manners. His hair is always faultlessly combed and parted, which compels me at once to realize that, in this important detail, I am very slovenly. His voice is as thin as a delicate twittering of birds. One involuntarily puts an arm around his shoulders when one goes for a walk with him, or when one speaks with him. He has no character, for he still has no idea at all what that is. Certainly he has not thought about life yet, and why should he think about it? He is very polite, ready to serve, and well-mannered, but without knowing it. Yes, he is like a bird. Cosiness comes out all over him. A bird gives one its hand when he does so, a bird walks like that and stands like that. Everything about Heinrich is innocent, peaceful, and happy. He wants to be a page, he says. But he says it without any indelicate wistfulness, and indeed the profession of page is thoroughly right and apt for him. The tenderness of his behavior and feeling aspires in some direction or other, and look, it reaches the right goal. What sort of experiences will he have? Will any experiences and any knowledge venture to approach this boy at all? Will not life's raw disappointments be too shy to upset him, him, with his pixie delicateness? I also observe that he is a little cold, there is nothing tempestuous and challenging about him. Perhaps he will not even notice many things that might have struck him low, and will not feel many things that might have robbed him of his blitheness. Who knows if I'm right! But I like, very very much, to make such observations. Heinrich is, to a certain extent, mindless. That is his good fortune, and one must allow him it. If he were a prince, I would be the first to bow my knee before him and make obeisance. What a pity!

How stupidly I behaved when I arrived here! Mainly I was shocked at the shabbiness of the front steps. Well, all right, they were just the stairs to an ordinary big-city back-street building. Then I rang the bell and a monkey-like being opened the door. It was Kraus. But at that time I simply thought of him as a monkey, whereas today I have a high opinion of him, because of the very personal quality which adorns him. I asked if I could speak to Herr Benjamenta. Kraus said: "Yes, sir!" and bowed to me, deeply and stupidly. This bow infused me with strange terror, for I told myself at once that there must be something wrong with the place. And from that moment, I regarded the Benjamenta school as a swindle. I went to the Principal's office. How I laugh when I think back on the scene that followed! Herr Benjamenta asked me what I wanted. I told him quietly that I wanted to become his pupil. At this, he fell silent and read newspapers. The office, the Principal, the monkey who led me in, the doors, the way of falling silent and reading newspapers, everything, everything seemed deeply suspicious to me, a promise of destruction. Suddenly I was asked for my name and where I came from. Now I thought I was lost, for suddenly I felt that I would never escape from the place. I stuttered out the information, I even ventured to emphasize that I came from a very good family. Among other things, I said that my father was an alderman, and that I had run away from him because I was afraid of being suf-focated by his excellence. Again the Principal fell silent for a while. My fear that I had been deceived grew most intense. I even thought of secret murder, of being slowly strangled. Then the Principal inquired, in his imperious voice, if I had any money with me, and I said that I had. "Give it to me, then. Quickly!" he commanded, and, strange to relate, I obeyed at once, although I was shaking with misery. I was now quite certain that I had fallen into the clutches of a robber and swindler, and all the same

I obediently laid the school fees down. How laughable my feelings at that time now seem to me! Then I found the heroic courage to ask, quietly, for a receipt, but I was given the following answer: "Rascals like you don't get receipts!" I almost fainted. The Principal rang a bell. Immediately the silly monkey Kraus rushed into the room. Silly monkey? Oh, not at all. Kraus is a dear, dear person. Only I understood no better at that time. "This is Jakob, the new pupil. Take him to the classroom." The Principal had hardly spoken when Kraus grabbed me and thrust me into the presence of the instructress. How childish one is when one is frightened! There is no worse behavior than that which comes from distrust and ignorance. That is how I became a pupil.

My school-friend Schacht is a strange person. He dreams of becoming a musician. He tells me that he plays the violin marvelously, with the help of his imagination, and I quite believe him. He likes to laugh, but then he lapses suddenly into wistful melancholy, which suits his face and bearing incredibly well. Schacht has a completely white face and long slender hands, which express a nameless suffering of soul. Being slight, as to the build of his body, he is easily all a-fidget, it is difficult for him to stand, or to sit, still. He is like a sickly, obstinate girl, he also likes grumbling, which makes him even more like a young and somewhat warped female being. He and I, we often lie together in my room on the bed, in our clothes, without taking our shoes off, and smoke cigarettes, which is against the rules. Schacht likes to offend against the rules and I, to be candid, unfortunately no less. We tell each other whole stories, when we are lying thus, stories from our lives, that is, experiences, but even more often invented stories, with the facts plucked from the air. When we do so, it seems to us that a soft music plays all up and down the walls. The narrow dark room expands, streets appear, palatial rooms, cities, châteaux, unknown people and landscapes, there are thunders and whisperings, voices speak and weep, et cetera. It is nice to talk to this slightly dreamy Schacht. He seems to understand everything that one tells him, and from time to time he says something significant himself. And then he often complains, and that is what I like about our conversation. I like hearing people complain. Then one can look just so at the person speaking, and have deep, intimate sympathy with him, and Schacht has something about him that rouses sympathy, even when he does not say depressing things. If there dwells in any man a delicate-minded dissatisfaction, that is, the yearning for something beautiful and lofty, it has made itself at home in Schacht. Schacht has a soul. Who knows, perhaps he has the disposition of an artist. He has confided to me that he is sick, and, since it is a question of a rather improper sickness, he has asked me urgently not to speak about it, which I have naturally promised, on my word of honor, in order to put his mind at rest. Then I asked him to show me the object of his malaise, but at that point he became a little angry and he turned to the wall. "You're terrible," he told me. Once I ventured to take his hand gently in mine, but he withdrew it and said: "What silliness are you up to now? Stop it." Schacht prefers to go about with me, this in particular I notice clearly, but in such matters clarity is not at all necessary. As a matter of fact, I like him enormously and regard him as an enrichment of my existence. Naturally I never told him such things. We say stupid things to each other, often serious things too, but avoiding big words. Fine words are much too boring. Ah, the meetings with Schacht in my room make me realize it: we pupils at the Ben-

jamenta Institute are condemned to a strange idleness, often last-
ing half the day. We always crouch, sit, stand, or lie around somewhere. Schacht and I often light candles in my room, for our en-
joyment. It is strictly forbidden. But that is why it is so much fun.
Whatever may be said in the rules: candlelight is so beautiful, so
mysterious. And how my friend's face looks when the small red
flame illuminates it! When I see candles burning, I always feel
that I am wealthy. The next moment, in comes the janitor and
gives me a scolding. That is all very senseless, but this senseless-
ness has a pretty mouth, and it smiles. Actually Schacht has coarse
features, but the pallor which suffuses his face refines them. His
nose is too big, so are his ears. His mouth is tight shut. Sometimes
when I see Schacht in this way I feel that this person will have a
bitterly hard time one day. How I love people who evoke this
mournful impression! Is that brotherly love? Yes, perhaps.

On the first day my behavior was enormously
prim, I was like mother's little boy. I was shown the room in
which I was to sleep together with the others, i.e., with Kraus,
Schacht, and Schilinski. A fourth to make up the party, as it were.
Everyone was there, my comrades, the Principal, who was looking
at me grimly, and his sister. Well, and then I simply threw myself
at the maiden's feet and exclaimed: "No, I can't sleep in that
room, it's impossible! I can't breathe in there. I'd rather spend the
night on the street." While I was speaking, I clung to the young
lady's legs. She seemed to be annoyed and told me to stand up. I
said: "I won't stand up until you promise to give me a decent
room to sleep in. I ask you, Fräulein, I implore you, put me somewhere else, in a hole, for all I care, but not in here. I can't be here.
I certainly won't offend my fellow-pupils, and if I've already done

so I'm sorry, but to sleep together with three people, as a fourth person, and in such a small room, too? It won't do. Ah, Fräulein!" She was smiling now, I noticed it, and so I quickly added, clinging even more tightly to her: "I'll be good, I promise you. I'll obey all your commands. You'll never, never have to complain of my behavior." Fräulein Benjamenta asked: "Is that so? Shall I never have to complain?" "No, it certainly isn't so, Fräulein," I replied. She exchanged a meaningful look with her brother, the Principal, and said to me: "Do please first stand up. Good heavens, what insistency and what a fuss! And now come along. You can sleep somewhere else, for all I care." She took me to the room in which I live now, showed it to me, and asked: "Do you like this room?" I was cheeky enough to say: "It's small. At home the windows had curtains. And the sun shone into the rooms there. Here there's only a narrow bed and a washstand. At home there were completely furnished rooms. But don't be angry Fräulein Benjamenta. I like it, and thank you. At home it was much more refined, friendlier and more elegant, but it's very nice here too. Forgive me for coming at you with the comparisons with how it was at home, and heaven knows what else besides. But I find the room very very charming. To be sure, the window up there in the wall can hardly be called a window. And the whole thing is definitely rather like a rat's hole, or a dog-kennel. But I like it. And I'm impertinent and ungrateful to talk to you like this, aren't I? Perhaps the best thing would be for you to take the room away from me again, though I have a really high opinion of it, and give me strict orders to sleep with the others. My comrades certainly feel offended. And you, Fräulein, are angry. I see it. It makes me very sad." She said to me: "You're a silly boy, and now you be quiet." And yet she was smiling. How silly it all was, on that first day. I was ashamed of myself, and I'm ashamed, to this day, when I think how improperly I behaved. I slept very restlessly the first night. I dreamed of the instructress. And as regards my own room, I would to this day be quite happy to share it with one or two other people. One is always half mad when one is shy of people.

Herr Benjamenta is a giant, and we pupils are dwarfs beside this giant, who is always rather gruff. As guide and commander of a crowd of such tiny, insignificant creatures as we boys are, he is certainly obliged, it is most natural, to be peevish, for this can never be a task that matches his powers: just ruling over us. No, Herr Benjamenta could do quite different things. Such a Hercules cannot help falling asleep, that is, growling and musing as he reads his newspapers, when he confronts such a petty exercise as that of educating us. What can the man have been thinking of when he decided to found the Institute? In a certain sense, it hurts me, and this feeling increases still more the respect that I have for him. Between him and me, at the beginning of my time here, I think it was during the morning of my second day, there was a small scene, but a violent one. I went into his office, but I couldn't manage to open my mouth. "Go outside again! See if it's possible for you to enter the room like a decent human being," he said austerely. I went out and then I knocked on the door, which I had quite forgotten to do before. "Come in," said a voice, and then I went in and stood there. "Well, aren't you going to make your bow? And what does one say on entering?" I bowed and said, in a feeble tone of voice: "Good day, Principal." Today I am so well trained that I positively trumpet out this "Good day, Principal." In those days, I hated this servile and polite way of behaving, it was just that I knew no better. What seemed to me laughable and dimwitted then, now seems apt and beautiful. "Speak louder, you rascal." exclaimed Herr Benjamenta. I had to repeat the greeting "Good day, Principal" five times. Only then did he ask what I wanted. I had got furious, and said: "One learns absolutely nothing here and I don't want to stay. Please give me my money back, and then I'll get out of the place. Where are the teachers here? Is there any plan, any idea to what we do? There's nothing. And I'm leaving. Nobody, whoever he is, will stop me from leaving this place of darkness and mystification. I come from much too good a family to let myself be plagued by your silly rules. To be sure, I don't mean to run back to my father and mother, never, but I'll take to the streets and sell myself as a slave. There's no harm in that." Well, I had said it. Today I almost have to double up with laughing when I recall this silly behavior. At that time, I felt altogether serious. But the Principal didn't say a word. I was on the verge of saying something rude and offensive to his face. Then he quietly spoke: "Sums of money, once paid in, are not paid back. As for your foolish opinion that you can learn nothing here, you are wrong, for you can learn. Learn, first of all, to know your surroundings. Your comrades are worth the attempt to get to know them. Talk with them. I advise you, keep calm. Nice and calm." This "nice and calm" he uttered as if in deep thought, without a care in the world for me. He kept his eyes downcast, as if he wanted me to understand how well and how gently he meant it. He gave me clear proofs of his being absent in thought, and was silent again. What could I do? Herr Benjamenta was already busy reading his newspapers again. I felt as if a terrible, incomprehensible storm was creeping up on me. I bowed deeply, almost to the ground, to him who was paying no more attention to me, said, as the rules required, "Adieu, Principal," clicked my heels, stood at attention, turned about, that is, no, I groped for the door handle, still kept looking at the Principal's face, and thrust myself, without turning around, through the door and out again. Thus ended my attempt at revolution. Since then, there have been no wilful scenes. My God, and I have been defeated. He defeated me, he, to whom I attribute a truly great heart, and I didn't move, didn't bat an eyelid, and he didn't even insult me. Only it hurt me, and not for my own sake, but for the Principal's. Actually, I am always thinking of him, of both of them, of him and Fräulein, the way they go on living here with us boys. What are they always doing in there, in their apartment? How do they keep themselves busy? Are they poor? Are the Benjamentas poor? There are "Inner Chambers" here. I have never been in them to this day. Kraus has, he is privileged, because he is so loyal. But Kraus doesn't want to give any information about the way the Principal's apartment is. He only goggles at me, when I ask him questions on this point, and says nothing. Oh, Kraus can really be silent. If I were a master, I would take Kraus into my service at once. But perhaps one day I shall penetrate into these inner chambers. And what will my eyes discover then? Perhaps nothing special at all? Oh, yes, something special. I know it, somewhere here there are marvelous things.

One thing is true, there is no nature here. That's just it, this is the big city, after all. At home there were views everywhere, near and far. I think I always heard the songbirds twittering up and down the streets. The streams were always murmuring. The woody mountain gazed down majestically upon the neat town. On the nearby lake one traveled, evenings, in a gondola. Cliffs and woods, hills and fields could be reached with a short walk. There were always voices and fragrances. And the streets of the town were like garden paths, they looked so soft and clean. Nice white houses peeped roguishly from green gardens. One saw well-known ladies, for example Frau Haag, out for a walk on the other side of the park fence. Silly it is, really, anyway nature, the mountain, the lake, the river, the foaming waterfall, the green foilage, and all sorts of songs and sounds were simply near at hand. If one went for a walk, it was like walking in the sky, for one saw blue sky everywhere. If one stood still, one could lie down straightaway and dream quietly up into the air, for there was grass or moss under one. And the pine trees that smell so wonderfully of spicy power. Shall I never see a mountain pine again? Really that would be no misfortune. To forgo something: that also has its fragrance and its power. Our alderman's house had no garden, but everything around was a neat, sweet, and pretty garden. I hope I am not yearning. Nonsense. It's good being here, too.

Although there's nothing much that merits a scrape, I run to the barber from time to time, for the sake of the excursion on the street, and have myself shaved. The barber's assistant asks if I am a Swede. An American? Not that either. A Russian? Well, then, what are you? I love to answer such nationalistically tinted questions with a steely silence, and to leave people who ask me about my patriotic feelings in the dark. Or I tell lies and say that I'm Danish. Some kinds of frankness are only hurtful and boring. Sometimes the sun shines like mad in these lively streets. Or everything is shrouded in rain, which I also very much like. The people are friendly, although I am unspeakably cheeky sometimes. Often in the lunch hour I sit idly on a bench. The trees in the park are quite colorless. The leaves hang down unnaturally,

like lead. Sometimes, it is as if everything here were made of metal
and thin iron. Then the rain descends and wets it all. Umbrellas
are opened, coaches rumble over the asphalt, people hurry, the
girls lift their skirts up. To see legs protruding from a skirt has
something peculiarly homey about it. A female leg like that, tightly
stockinged, one never sees, and now suddenly one sees it. The
shoes cling so beautifully to the shape of the beautiful soft feet.
Then the sun is shining again. A little wind blows, and then one
thinks of home. Yes, I think of Mamma. She will be crying. Why
don't I ever write to her? I can't tell why, can't understand it, and
yet I can't decide to write. That's it: I don't want to tell anything.
It's too silly. A pity, I shouldn't have parents who love me. I
don't want to be loved and desired at all. They will have to get
used to not having a son any more.

To be of service to somebody whom one does
not know, and who has nothing to do with one, that is charming,
it gives one a glimpse into divine and misty paradises. Even then:
all people, or almost all, have something to do with one. The
people passing by, they have something to do with me, that's for
sure. Of course, it's really a private affair. I walk along, the sun is
shining, then suddenly I see a puppy whimpering at my feet. At
once I observe that this little animal extravagance has got his small
legs caught up in his muzzle. He can't walk any more. I stoop and
this great big misfortune is a thing of the past. Now the dog's mistress comes marching along. She sees what has happened, and
thanks me. Fleetingly I doff my hat to the lady and I go on my
way. Ah, that lady back there is now thinking that there are still
polite young men in the world. Well and good. I have been of service to young people in general. And how this woman (she was not

unpretty) smiled at me. "Thank you, sir." Ah, she made me a Sir.
Yes, when one knows how to behave, one is a Sir. And when one
says thank you, one respects the person whom one is thanking. The
person who smiles is pretty. All women deserve politeness. Every
woman has something refined about her. I have seen washerwomen
who moved like queens. That is all comical, oh, so comical. And
how the sun shone, and then how I ran off!—off into the shop:
I'm getting myself photographed there. Herr Benjamenta wants a
photograph of me. And then I must write a short and true account
of my life. That means paper. So I have the added pleasure of
walking into a stationer's.

Comrade Schilinski comes from a Polish family.
He speaks an attractive broken German. Everything that is foreign
sounds noble, I don't know why. Schilinski's great pride is an
electric tiepin that he got hold of somehow. He also likes, very
much indeed, striking wax matches. Remarkably often one sees
him cleaning his suit, polishing his boots and brushing his cap. He
likes to look at himself in a cheap pocket mirror. Of course, we
pupils have all got pocket mirrors, although we really do not know
the meaning of vanity. Schilinski is slim and has an attractive face
and curly hair, which he tirelessly combs and tends during the
day. He says he would like to have a pony. To comb and groom a
horse, and then go out on it, is his fondest dream. His mental gifts
are few and far between. He is not quick-witted at all, one should
not, in his case, speak of subtlety of mind. And yet he is not at all
stupid, limited perhaps, but I don't like to use this word when
thinking of my school-friends. That I am the cleverest of them all
is perhaps not altogether so very delightful. What is the use of
thoughts and ideas if one feels, as I do, that one doesn't know

what to do with them? Anyway. No, no, I'll try to see things clearly and I don't want to be hoitytoity, I never want to feel superior to my surroundings. Schilinski will have good luck in life. Women will prefer him, that is how he looks, altogether the future darling of women. His face and hands have a light-brownish complexion, which reminds one of something distinguished, and his eyes are bashful as a doe's. They are charming eyes. He could be the perfect young country nobleman. His behavior reminds one of a country estate, where city and peasant life, the refined and the rough, commingle in graceful and strong human culture. He likes especially to stroll idly around, and in the liveliest streets, where I sometimes accompany him, to the horror of Kraus, who hates idleness and persecutes and scorns it. "So you two have been out having fun again, have you?"—that's how Kraus welcomes us when we come back home. I shall have much to say about Kraus. He is the most honest and efficient of us pupils, and efficiency and honesty are inexhaustible and immeasurable domains. Nothing can excite me so deeply as the sight and smell of what is good and just. You soon reach the end of feeling about vulgar and evil things, but to get wise to something good and noble is so difficult, and yet also so alluring. No, vices do not interest me much, much less than the virtues. Now I shall have to describe Kraus and I'm positively scared of doing so. Pruderies? Since when? I hope not.

I now go every day to the shop and ask if my photographs will not be ready soon. Each time, I can go up to the top floor in the elevator. I find that rather nice, and it matches my many other inanities. When I travel in an elevator, I really do feel that I am a child of my times. Do other people find it so? I haven't written the account of my life yet. It embarrasses me a

little to tell the simple truth about my past. Kraus looks at me
more and more reproachfully every day. That suits me very well.
I like to see people I love getting a little angry. Nothing pleases me
more than to give a completely false image of myself to people for
whom I have made a place in my heart. Perhaps that's unjust,
but it is audacious, so it is right. Of course, it is a little morbid, in
my case. Thus, for example, I imagine that it would be unspeakably lovely to die with the terrible knowledge that I have offended
whomsoever I love the most and have filled them with bad opinions of me. Nobody will understand that, or only someone who can
sense tremblings of beauty in defiance. To die miserably, because
of some mischeif, some silliness. Isn't that desirable? No, certainly
not. But these are all sillinesses of the crassest kind. At this point
something occurs to me and I see myself compelled, for some unknown reason, to say it. A week or more ago I still had ten marks.
Well, now these ten marks are gone. One day I walked into a
restaurant, one with hostesses. I was quite irresistibly drawn into
the place. A girl leaped toward me and forced me to sit down on
a sofa. I half knew how it would end. I resisted, but without the
slightest emphasis. I just didn't care, and yet I did. It was pleasure
beyond compare to play to the girl the role of the refined and
condescending gentleman. We were quite alone, and we did the
nicest of silly things. We drank. She kept running to the bar, to
fetch new drinks. She showed me her charming garter and I
caressed it with my lips. Ah, how silly one is. She kept standing
up and fetching new things to drink. And so quickly. It was just
that she wanted to earn a nice little sum of money from the silly
boy. I know this perfectly well, but it was precisely this that I
liked—her thinking me silly. Such a peculiar vice: to be secretly
pleased to be allowed to observe that one is being slightly robbed.

But how enchanting it all seemed to me. All around me, everything was fading out in fluting, caressing music. The girl was Polish, slim and supple, and so deliciously sinful. I thought: "There go my ten marks." So I kissed her. She said: "Tell me, what are you? You behave like a nobleman." I was gulping my fill of the fragrance that flowed from her. She noticed it and thought it was refined. And in fact: what sort of a scoundrel would go, without any feeling for love and beauty, to places where only delight forgives what depravity has undertaken? I lied and said that I was a stableboy. She said: "Oh, no, you behave much too beautifully to be that. Now say Hello." And so I did what they call Saying Hello in such places, that is, she explained it to me, laughing and joking and kissing me, and then I did it. A moment later I found myself on the evening street, cleaned out, down to the last penny. How do I feel about that now? I don't know. But one thing I do know: I must get hold of some money. But how shall I do that?

Almost every early morning there begins a duel of whisperings between Kraus and me. Kraus always believes that he must spur me on to work. Perhaps he's not entirely wrong in supposing that I do not like to get up early. I certainly do like getting up early, but I also find it quite delicious to lie in bed a little longer than I should. To be supposed not to do something is so alluring sometimes that one cannot help doing it. Therefore I love so deeply every kind of compulsion, because it allows me to take joy in what is illicit. If there were no commandments, no duties in the world, I would die, starve, be crippled by boredom. I only have to be spurred on, compelled, regimented. It suits me entirely. Ultimately it is I who decides, only I. I provoke the frowning law to anger a little, afterwards I make the effort to pacify it. Kraus is the embodiment of all the rules here in the Benja-menta Institute, consequently I am always challenging the best of all my fellow-pupils to somewhat of a struggle. I would get ill if I could not quarrel, and Kraus is wonderfully well-suited for quarreling and teasing. He is always right: "Now it really is time you got up, you lazy rat!" And I am always wrong: "Yes, yes, patience, I'm coming." A person in the wrong is cheeky enough always to challenge the patience of a person in the right. Being right is heated, being wrong always makes a show of proud, frivolous composure. The one who is so passionately well-meaning (Kraus) is always defeated by the one (me) who is not so outspokenly intent on what is good and requisite. I triumph, because I carry on lying in bed, and Kraus quakes with wrath, because he has to keep knocking vainly on the door, stamping his foot and saying: "Get up now, Jakob! Do it now! God, what a lazybones." Ah, I do like people who can get angry. Kraus gets angry on the slightest pretext. That is so beautiful, so humorous, so noble. And we two suit one another so well. The sinner must always be faced with the person outraged, or else something would be missing. Then once I have finally got up, I act as if I were standing idly around. "There he is now, standing and gaping, the ninny, instead of doing something," he says then. How splendid that sort of thing is. The mumbling of a grumbler is lovelier to me than the murmuring of a woodland stream, with the loveliest of Sunday morning sunshine sparkling on it. People, people, nothing but people! Yes, I feel it most strongly: I love people. Their follies and sudden excitements are more dear and valuable to me than the subtlest wonders of nature.—We pupils have to sweep and clean the classroom and the office early in the morning, before our superiors wake up. Two of us do it, in turns. "Get up now. Are you ready yet?" Or: "You won't be so satisfied with yourself for long." Or: "Get up, get up. It's time. You should have had the broom in your hand long ago." How amusing this is! And Kraus, eternally angry Kraus, how fond of him I am.

Once again I must go back to the very beginning, to the first day. In the break, Schacht and Schilinski, whom I did not know at that time, ran into the kitchen and brought breakfast, laid on plates, into the classroom. I also was given something to eat, but I wasn't hungry, I didn't want to touch any of it. "You must eat," Schacht said to me, and Kraus added: "Everything on the plate has to be eaten up, everything. Do you understand?" I still remember how repulsive I found those words. I tried to eat, but disgustedly left most of it. Kraus came through the crowd to me and clapped me dignifiedly on the shoulder and said: "You're new here, but you must understand that the rules insist on all food being eaten up. You're proud, but wait a while, you'll soon lose your pride. Can you pick buttered bread and slices of sausage off the street? Can you? Wait a while and see, perhaps you'll get an appetite. Anyway, you must eat up all this here, that's for certain. In the Benjamenta Institute no leftovers are tolerated. Get on with it, eat. Quickly. What anxious hesitation, I suppose you think you're so refined! You'll soon lose your refinements, I can tell you. You've no appetite, you say? But I advise you to have one. It's because of pride that you haven't got one, that's what it is. Give it here! This time I'll help you to eat it up, though it's all against the rules. Right. Now you see how one can eat it? And this? And that? That was clever, I can tell you." How embarrassed I was. I felt a violent aversion to this eating boy, and today? Today I eat everything up as tidily as any of the pupils. I even look forward every time to the nicely prepared and modest meals, and it would never occur to me to disdain them. Yes, I was vain and proud at the start, offended by I don't know what, humiliated I no longer know how. Everything, everything was still simply new to me, and, consequently, hostile, and besides, I was a wholly outstanding fool. I am a fool to this day, but in a way that is finer and friendlier. And everything depends on the way a thing is. A person can be utterly foolish and unknowing: as long as he knows the way to adapt, to be flexible, and how to move about, he is still not lost, but will come through life better perhaps than someone who is clever and stuffed with knowledge. The way: yes, yes.

Kraus has had a hard life, even before he came here. He and his father, who is a boatman, traveled up and down the Elbe, on heavy coal barges. He had to work hard, hard, until one day he fell ill. Now he wants to be a servant, a real servant, to some master, and it's as if he was born for it, with all his good-hearted qualities. He will be a quite wonderful servant, for not only does his appearance suit this profession of humility and obligingness, no, also his soul, his whole nature, the whole human character of my friend has, in the best sense, something servant-like about it. To serve! If only Kraus can find a decent master, I wish that for him. There certainly are gentlemen, or lords, in brief, superiors, who do not like or wish to be served perfectly, who do not know how to accept real achievements of service. Kraus has style and he definitely belongs to a Count, that is, to an entirely distinguished gentleman. One should not let Kraus work like an ordinary laborer or worker. He can be a representative. His face is perfect for indicating a certain tone, a manner, and anyone hiring him can be proud of his bearing and his behavior. Hire him! Yes, that is the expression people use. And one day Kraus will be hired out to somebody, or hired by somebody. And he is looking forward to it, and that is why he is so zealously stowing French away in his somewhat slow head. There's something about his head that troubles him. At the barber's, so he says, he acquired a rather horrid mark of distinction, a garland of small reddish plants, or briefly, points, or, even more briefly, and unmercifully, spots. Anyway, that's bad, of course, especially since he wants to go to a fine and really decent master. What's to be done? Poor Kraus! The points that disfigure him would not prevent me, for example, from kissing him if it came to such a pass, not at all. Seriously: they really would not, for I don't notice such things any more, I no longer see that it looks unbeautiful. I see his beautiful soul in his face, and it is the soul that most deserves to be caressed. But the future lord and master will, of course, think quite differently, and that is also why Kraus puts ointments on his inelegant wounds, which disfigure him. Also he often uses the mirror to observe the progress of the treatment, not out of empty vanity. If he didn't have these blemishes, he would never look into a mirror, for the earth cannot produce anything more unvain, uninflated, than him. Herr Benjamenta, who has a lively interest in Kraus, often inquires about the evil and its hoped-for disappearance. For Kraus will soon be going out into life and into a job. I'm afraid of the moment when he will leave the school. But it won't come all that soon. He can still spend quite a long time doctoring his face, I believe, which I don't wish to be the case, and yet I do wish it. He will come to his master quite soon enough, to one who will know how to prize his qualities, and soon enough I shall have to do without a person whom I love, without his knowing it.

I write all these lines mostly in the evening, by the lamplight, at the big school table, at which, obtusely or not obtusely, we pupils so often have to sit. Kraus is sometimes very inquisitive and looks over my shoulder. Once I corrected him: "But Kraus, tell me, since when have you been bothering about things that don't concern you?" He was very annoyed, as all people are when they are caught on the secret pathways of stealthy curiosity. Sometimes I sit idly quite alone until late in the night on a bench in the public garden. The streetlights are on, the garish electric light descends, liquid and burning, among the leaves of the trees. Everything is hot and promises strange intimacies. People walk back and forth. Whisperings come from the hidden paths of the park. Then I go home and find the door closed. "Schacht," I call softly, and my comrade, as arranged, throws me the key down into the courtyard. I creep on tiptoe, since it is forbidden to stay out for long, into my room, and go to bed. And then I dream. I often dream terrible things. Thus one night I dreamed that I struck my mother in the face, my dear mother, far away. What a scream I gave, and how suddenly I woke up. Pain at the dreadfulness of what I had done chased me out of bed. I had seized the holy one by her respect-arousing hair and had thrown her to the ground. Oh, not to think of such things. The tears shot like sharp jets from the motherly eyes. I still clearly remember how the misery cut and tore her mouth, and how engulfed in sorrow she was, and how her head then sank back. But why recall these images again? Tomorrow I shall finally have to write the account of my life, or I shall be in peril of a severe reproof. In the evenings, at about nine o'clock, we boys always sing a short goodnight song. We stand in a semicircle by the door that leads to the inner chambers, and then the door opens, Fräulein Benjamenta appears on the threshold, clad all in wholesomely flowing white robes, and says to us, "Good night, boys," orders us to go to sleep now, and warns us to be quiet. Then, each time, Kraus puts out the lamp in the schoolroom, and from this moment not the slightest sound may be made. Everyone has to go on tiptoe to his bed. It is all quite peculiar. And where do the Benjamentas sleep? The Fräulein looks like an angel when she says goodnight to us. How I revere her! In the evening the Principal is never to be seen. Whether that is peculiar or not, it is certainly conspicuous.

It seems that the Benjamenta Institute once had more of a reputation and more customers than now. On one of the four walls of our classroom hangs a large photograph, with portraits of a great number of boys who attended the school during a previous year. Apart from that, our classroom is very sparsely equipped. Apart from the longish table, about ten or twelve chairs, a big wall-cupboard, an old traveling trunk, and a few other negligible objects, it has no furniture. Over the door which leads into the secret, unknown world of inner chambers, there hangs as a wall decoration a rather tedious-looking policeman's saber with an equally tedious-looking sheath laid across it. The helmet is enthroned above them. This decoration is like a sign, or like delicate evidence, of the rules that prevail here. As for me, I wouldn't accept these adornments if I were made a present of them; probably they were bought from an old junk-dealer. Every fortnight saber and helmet are taken down to be cleaned, which, it must be said, is a very nice but certainly altogether stupid job. Beside these ornaments there hang in the classroom the pictures of the late Emperor and Empress. The old Emperor looks unbelievably peaceful, and the Empress has a simple, motherly look. Often we pupils wash out the classroom with soap and hot water, so that afterwards everything smells and shines with cleanliness. We have to do everything ourselves, and each of us has for this housemaid's work an apron around his waist, in which garment, with its redolence of femininity, we all without exception look comical. But we have a merry time on such cleaning days. The floor is gaily polished, the objects, also those in the kitchen, are rubbed until they shine, for which purpose there are dusters and cleaning powders in plenty. Tables and chairs are smothered in water, door handles are polished till they gleam, windowpanes are breathed on and rubbed clean, each of us has his little task, each of us does something. On such days of cleaning, rubbing, and washing, we are like the elves in fairy tales, who, as is known, used to do all their rough and laborious tasks out of pure, supernatural goodness of heart. What we pupils do, we do because we have to, but why we have to, nobody quite knows. We obey, without considering what will one day come of all this thoughtless obedience, and we work without thinking if it is right and good to do our work. On one such cleaning day, Tremala, the oldest of us all, came up to me and tried an ugly trick. He stood quietly behind me and reached with his disgusting hand (hands that do this are crude and disgusting) for my intimate member, with the intention of doing me a loathsome favor, almost like tickling an animal. I turn around quickly and knock the villain to the floor. Usually I'm not so strong, Tremala is much stronger. But anger gave me irresistible strength. Tremala drags himself to his feet and hurls himself at me, then the door opens and Herr Benjamenta is standing in the doorway. "Jakob, you rascal!" he calls, "come here!" I go to my Principal and he doesn't ask at all who started the fight, but gives me a slap on the head and walks off. I'm about to run after him and shout at him how unjust he is, but I control myself, think, look over at the whole crowd of boys, and go back to my work. Since then I haven't spoken a word to Tremala, and he also avoids me, he knows why. But whether he's sorry, or anything like that, doesn't matter to me. The indelicate incident has long been, how shall I say, forgotten. In earlier times, Tremala has been to sea in ships. He's a depraved person, and rejoices in his vile tendencies. Also he is frantically uncultivated, therefore he doesn't interest me. Sly, and at the same time incredibly stupid: how uninteresting! But Tremala has taught me one thing: one must always be somewhat on the lookout for all kinds of assaults and injuries.

Often I go out onto the street, and there I seem to be living in an altogether wild fairy tale. What a crush and a crowd, what rattlings and patterings! What shoutings, whizzings, and hummings! And everything so tightly penned in. Right up close to the wheels of cars people are walking, children, girls, men, and elegant women; old men and cripples and people with bandaged heads, one sees all these in the crowd. And always fresh bevies of people and vehicles. The coaches of the electric trolleys look like boxfuls of figures. The buses go galumphing past like clumsy great beetles. Then there are wagons that look like traveling watchtowers. People sit on the seats high up and travel over the heads of whatever is walking, jumping, and running below. Fresh crowds thrust in among the existing ones, and all at the same time there's a going and a coming, an appearing and a vanishing. Horses trample. Wonderful hats with ornamental feathers nod from open, swiftly-passing rich folks' coaches. All Europe sends its human specimens here. Gentility walks cheek by jowl with the menial and the bad, people are going who knows where, and here they come again and they are quite different people and who knows where they are coming from. One thinks that one can untangle it all a little, and one is glad to be taking the trouble to do so. And the sun sparkles down on it all. It shines on one person's nose, on another's toecap. Lacework pokes from the hems of skirts in a glittering confusion. Small dogs go riding on the laps of genteel old women in coaches. Breasts bounce toward one, female breasts pressed into clothes and shapes. And then again there are the many silly cigars in the many slits of masculine mouthparts. And one thinks of undreamed-of streets, invisible new regions, equally swarming with people. Evenings, between six and eight, the swarming is most graceful and dense. At this hour the best society goes promenading. What is one, really, in this flood, in this various, never-ending river of people? Sometimes all these mobile faces are reddishly tinted and painted by the glow of the setting sun. And when it is grey and raining? Then all these figures, and myself among them, walk quickly along like images in a dream under the dark gauze, looking for something and, it seems, almost never finding anything that is beautiful and right. Everyone is looking for something here, everyone is longing to be rich and to possess the fabulous goods of fortune. One walks quickly. No, they all restrain themselves, but the haste, the longing, the torment, and the restlessness gleam out of their greedy eyes. Then again everything swims in the hot noonday sun. Everything seems to be asleep, even the vehicles, the horses, the wheels, the noises. And the people look so blank. The tall, apparently collapsing houses seem to be dreaming. Girls hurry along, parcels are carried. One would like to fling one's arms around somebody. When I come home, Kraus sits there and makes fun of me. I tell him that one really must get to know the world a little. "Know the world?" he says, as if immersed in deep thought. And he smiles scornfully.

About a fortnight after my arrival at the school, Hans appeared among us. Hans is a regular peasant boy, like the ones in the Grimms' fairy tales. He comes from deepest Mecklenburg, and he smells of flowery, luxuriant meadows, of cow barn and farmyard. He is slim, rough, and bony, and he speaks a strange, goodhearted peasant language, which I like, as a matter of fact, if I take the trouble to hold my nose. Not that Hans gives off bad smells or anything. And yet one does hold some kind of a nose, perhaps a mental one, a cultural nose or soul nose, and one can't help doing so, without even wanting to offend the good Hans. And he doesn't notice such things at all, this country person sees and hears and feels in far too healthy and plain a way for that. Something like the earth itself and earth-furrows and curves confronts one, when one looks deeply into this boy, but there's no need to look deeply. Hans doesn't demand pensiveness. Not that he doesn't matter to me, not that at all, but, how shall I say, he is a little remote and lightweight. One takes him quite lightly, because nothing about him gives serious cause for emotion. The Grimms' Fairy Tale Peasant Boy. Old-fashioned and agreeable, understandable and essential at the first fleeting glance. Very worthwhile to be a good friend to the fellow. In later life, Hans will work hard, without sighing. He will hardly notice the exertions, worries, and adversities. He is bursting with strength and health. And yet he's not bad-looking. Altogether: I can't help laughing at myself: I find something slightly nice in everything and about everything. I like them all so much, my pupils here, my school-friends.

Am I a born city dweller? It's quite possible. I hardly ever get stunned or surprised. There's something unspeakably cool about me, in spite of the excitements that can attack me. I have shed provincial habits in six days. Of course, I did grow up in a very very small metropolis. I drank in city life and city feeling with my mother's milk. As a child I saw yowling drunken workers reeling about. Even when I was very small, nature seemed to me a remote heaven. So I can do without nature. Doesn't one then have to do without God, too? To know that goodness, pure and sublime, is hidden somewhere, somewhere in the mists, and to revere and adore it very very quietly, with an ardor that is, as it were, totally cool and shadowy: I'm accustomed to that. One day as a child I saw an Italian workman lying dead against a wall, in a pool of blood, and pierced by numerous knife-wounds. And another time, it was in the days of Ravachol, we young people told each other that bombs would soon be getting thrown in our part of the world as well, et cetera. Old times, those. I meant to talk of something quite different, that is, of comrade Peter, Beanpole Peter. This exceedingly tall boy is too funny, he comes from Teplitz in Bohemia and can speak Slavic and German. His father is a policeman, and Peter was trained as a clerk in a rope works, but he seems to have played being ignorant, unusable, and unsuccessful, which I, privately, find very endearing. He says that he can also speak Hungarian and Polish, if it is asked of him. But here nobody asks any such thing of him. What extensive knowledge of languages! Peter is quite decidedly the silliest and the clumsiest of us pupils, and that heaps him and wreathes him with distinctions in my inconsiderable eyes, for I am unbelievably fond of silly people. I hate the kind of person who pretends he understands everything and beamingly parades knowledge and wit. Sly and knowing people are to me an unspeakable abomination. How nice Peter is, in precisely this point. His being tall, so tall that he could crack in two, is good, but even better is the goodness of heart which keeps whispering to him that he is a cavalier and has the looks of a noble and elegant rake. It's a great laugh. He's always talking of adventures he has had, but probably hasn't had. Anyway, one thing is true: Peter owns the finest and most delicate walking stick in the world. And now he is always going out and walking the liveliest streets with this stick in his hand. Once I met him in the F—— Street. F—— Street is the fascinating focus of cosmopolitan life in this big city. Still a long way off, he was waving his hand to me nodding and brandishing his walking stick. Then, when I was close to him, he looked paternally and anxiously at me, as if to say: "What? You here too? Jakob, Jakob, this is no place for you." And then he took his leave, like one of the great men of the world, like the editor of an internationally famous newspaper who can't spare a moment of his highly valuable time. And then I saw his round, silly, nice little hat vanishing in the mass of other heads and hats. He melted, as they say, into the crowd. Peter learns absolutely nothing, although in his so humorous way he really needs to, and it seems that he only came to the Benjamenta Institute in order to distinguish himself with the most delightful sillinesses. Perhaps he's even becoming a few considerable degrees sillier than he was, and why, indeed, shouldn't his silliness be allowed to develop? I, for instance, am convinced that Peter will have a shameful amount of success in life, and, strange to say, I grant him this. Yes, I even go further. I have the feeling, and it is a very comforting one, tingling and pleasant, that I shall one day obtain a master, lord, and superior such as Peter would be, for such silly people

are made for promotion, advancement, good living, and the giving of commands, and such people as I am, to some extent intelligent, should let the good impulses which they possess blossom and
exhaust themselves in the service of others. Me, I shall be something very lowly and small. The feeling that tells me this is like a
complete and inviolable fact. My God, and do I have, all the same,
so much, so much zest for life? What is it with me? Often I'm a
little frightened of myself, but not for long. No, no, I have confidence in myself. But isn't that altogether comic?

For my fellow-pupil Fuchs I have only one single
expression: Fuchs is crosswise, Fuchs is askew. He speaks like a
flopped somersault and behaves like a big improbability pummeled
into human shape. Everything about him is unpleasant, therefore
unlovable. To know something about Fuchs is an abuse, a coarse
and bothersome superfluity. One only knows such rascals in order
to despise them; but since one doesn't want in the least to despise
anything, one forgets and overlooks it. It, yes. For an it is what he
is, a thing. O God, why must I talk angrily today? I could almost
hate myself for it. Away to something better.—I see Herr Benjamenta very rarely. Sometimes I go into the office, bow to the
ground, say, "Good day, Principal," and ask this kingly man if
I may go out. "Have you written the account of your life, eh?" I
am asked. I reply: "Not yet. But I shall do so." Herr Benjamenta
comes up to me, that is, up to the counter at which I'm standing,
and pushes his gigantic fist up to my nose. "You'll be on time with
it, boy, or else—you know what comes of that." I understand him,
I bow again and disappear. Curious, the pleasure it gives me to
annoy practicers of force. Do I actually want this Herr Benjamenta to punish me? Do I have reckless instincts? Everything is

possible, everything, even the most sordid and undignified things. Very well, then, soon I shall write the account of my life. I find Herr Benjamenta very handsome indeed. A glorious brown beard —what? Glorious brown beard? I'm a fool. No, there's nothing handsome about the Principal, nothing glorious, but behind this man one senses difficult paths of destiny and heavy blows of fate, and it is this human thing, this almost divine thing, that makes him handsome. True people and true men are never visibly handsome. A man who has a really handsome beard is an opera singer or a well-paid departmental chief in a big store. Surface people are handsome, as a rule. However, there may be exceptions and specimens of masculine handsomeness that are authentic. Herr Benjamenta's face and hands (I have already felt his hand) are like knotty roots, roots which at some sad moment have had to withstand a few unmerciful ax-blows. If I were a lady of noblesse and intelligence, I would know absolutely how to bestow distinction on men like this apparently so impecunious principal of an institute, but, as I suppose, Herr Benjamenta doesn't mix with society on the worldly stage. Actually he is always at home, doubtless he keeps sort of hidden away, he creeps away, "into the solitude," and, indeed, this noble and clever man must live a horribly lonely life. Something must have happened to make on this character a deep and perhaps even destructive impression, but who knows? A pupil at the Benjamenta Institute, whatever can such a person know? But at least I am always investigating. In order to investigate, I often go to the office for no other reason than to ask the man just such fiddling questions as this "May I go out, Principal?" Yes, this man has a fascination for me, he interests me. The instructress also arouses my most intense interest. Yes, and for this reason, to get something out of all this mystery, I irritate him so that something like an incautious remark may escape from him. What's the harm if he hits me? My desire for experiences is growing into a domineering passion, and the pain which this strange man's annoyance causes me is small in comparison with my trembling wish to lead him on into saying something a little revealing. Oh, I dream—glorious, glorious—of winning the confidence which this man is just beginning to show. It may take a long time, but I think, I think I shall manage to penetrate at last the mystery of the Benjamentas. Mysteries make one dream of unendurable bewitchments, they have the fragrance of something quite, quite unspeakably beautiful. Who knows, who knows. Ah—

I love the noise and restless movement of the city. Perpetual motion compels morality. A thief, for example, when he sees all the bustling people, would not be able to help thinking what a scoundrel he is, and then the blithe and brisk sight of it all can feed betterment into his crumbling, ruin-like character. The braggart will perhaps become more modest and thoughtful when he catches sight of all the forces at work here, and this unseemly fellow may tell himself, when the supple throngs catch his attention, that he must be a dreadful rogue to set himself up, stupidly and vainly, with such conceit and arrogance. The city educates, it cultivates, and by examples, what's more, not by arid precepts from books. There is nothing professorial about it, and that is flattering, for the towering gravity of knowledge discourages one. And then there is so much here that fosters, sustains, and helps. One can hardly express it. How difficult it is to give living expression to that which is fine and good! One is grateful, here, for one's morsel of life, one is always a little grateful, while it is urging one on, while one is in a hurry. A person with time to waste doesn't know what time means, and he is the natural stupid ingrate. In the city, there isn't a messenger boy who doesn't know the value of his time, there isn't a newsboy who trifles his time away. And then how dreamlike it is, picturesque and poetic! People keep scuttling and shoving by. Well, now, that's important, that is stimulating, that gives the mind a more zestful rhythm. While one is standing hesitantly around, a hundred people and a hundred things have passed through one's head and before one's eyes, which proves very clearly what a dawdler and a sluggard one is. There is such a general hurry here because people think every moment how nice it is to go struggling and grasping for things. The breath of life becomes more bewitching. The wounds and pains go deeper, joy jubilates more joyously and for longer than elsewhere, because anyone who is joyous here always seems to have bitterly and justly earned it by hard toil. Then again there are the gardens that lie behind the delicate fencings, so quiet and lost, like secret corners in English parklands. Right beside them the business traffic rushes by and clatters past, as if landscapes or dreams had never existed. The railway trains thunder over the quivering bridges. Evenings, the fabulous rich and elegant shop-windows shine, and streams, serpents, and billows of people roll past the allures of industrial riches on display. Yes, that all seems grand and good to me. One profits from being in the midst of the whirling and bubbling. One has a good feeling in the legs, the arms, and the chest while making the effort to wriggle cleverly and without much fuss through all the living stuff. In the morning everything comes to life anew, and in the evening everything sinks into the wildly embracing arms of a new and unknown dream. That's very poetic. Fräulein Benjamenta would quite rightly admonish me if she were to read what I am writing here. Not to speak of Kraus, who makes no such passionate distinction between village and city. Kraus sees, firstly, people, second, duties, and third, at the most, savings which he will put aside, he thinks, to send to his mother. Kraus always writes home. He has an education that is as simple as it is purely human. The turmoil of the big city with all its many foolish, glittering promises leaves him completely cold. What an upright, tender, solid human soul!

At last my photographs are finished. The portrait, a really good one, shows me looking out very very energetically into the world. Kraus tries to annoy me and says that I look like a Jew. At last, at last he laughs a bit. "Kraus," I say, "please realize, even Jews are people." We quarrel about the worth and worthlessness of the Jews and it is splendid entertainment. I wonder what good opinions he has: "The Jews have all the money," he thinks. I nod, I agree and say: "It's money that makes people Jews. A poor Jew isn't a Jew, and rich Christians, they're dreadful, they're the worst Jews of all." He nods. At last, at last I have found this person's approval. But now he's angry again and says very gravely: "Stop this gabbling! What's all this about Jews and Christians? Such people don't exist. There are mean people and good ones. That's all. And what do you think about that, Jakob? Which sort are you?" And now a really long discussion starts. Oh, Kraus likes to talk with me very much, I know it. The good, fine soul. Only he doesn't want to admit it. How I love people who don't like making admissions! Kraus has character: how clearly one feels that.—Of course, I've written the account of my life, but I tore it up. Fräulein Benjamenta warned me yesterday to be more attentive and obedient. I have the loveliest ideas about obedience and attentiveness, and it's strange: they escape me. I am virtuous in my imagination, but when it comes to practicing virtue? What then? You see, then it's quite another matter, then one fails, then one is reluctant. Also I am impolite. I long very much to be courtly and polite, but when it's a question of speeding ahead of the instructress and opening the door for her respectfully, who's that scoundrel there, sitting at the table? And who springs up like a gale to show his manners? Aha, it's Kraus. Kraus is a knight from head to toe. Truly, he belongs in the Middle Ages, and it really is a pity that he hasn't got a Twelfth Century at his disposal. He is fidelity in person, ardent service and unobtrusive, selfless obligingness. He has no judgment about women, he merely respects them. Who lifts from the floor what has fallen there, and hands it quick as a squirrel to the lady? Who leaps from the house on errands? Who carries the shopping bag when the instructress goes to market? Who scrubs the stairs and the kitchen without being told? Who does all this and doesn't ask for thanks? Who is so gloriously, so powerfully happy in himself? What is his name? Ah, I know who it is. Sometimes I'd like this Kraus to punch me. But people like him, how could they punch? Kraus only wants what is right and good. That is no exaggeration at all. He never has bad intentions. His eyes are frighteningly kind. This person, what is he really doing in a world that is meant and built for empty words, lies, and vanity? When one looks at Kraus, one can't help feeling how hopelessly lost in the world modesty is.

I have sold my watch, so as to buy tobacco for cigarettes. I can live without a watch, but not without cigarettes, that is shameful, but a necessity. Somehow I must get some money or I shan't have any clean clothes to wear. Clean collars are things I can't do without. A person's happiness depends, yet does not depend, on such things. Happiness? No. But one should be proper. Cleanliness alone is a joy. I'm just talking. How I hate all the right words! Today the Fräulein cried. Why? Halfway through the class, tears suddenly poured from her eyes. It strangely moves me. Anyway, I shall have to keep my eyes peeled. I like listening for something that doesn't want to make a sound. I pay attention, and that makes life more beautiful, for if we don't have to pay attention there really is no life. It is clear, Fräulein Benjamenta is grieving and it must be a violent grief, because usually our instructress is very self-controlled. I must get some money. And another thing: I've written the account of my life. This is how it goes:

MY LIFE

The undersigned, Jakob von Gunten, son of honorable parents, born on such and such a day, raised in such and such a place, entered the Benjamenta Institute as a pupil in order to acquire knowledge of the few things necessary for entering someone's service. The same has no high hopes of life. He wishes to be treated strictly, so that he may know what it means to pull himself together. Jakob von Gunten is not very promising, but he proposes to behave well and honestly. The von Guntens are an old family. In earlier times they were warriors, but their pugnacity has diminished and today they are aldermen and tradesmen, and the youngest of the house, subject of this report, has resolved to lapse from every proud tradition. He wants life to educate him, not inherited or noble principles. Of course, he is proud, for it is impossible for him to deny his inborn nature, but by pride he means something quite new, something that corresponds, in some degree, to the times in which he is living. He hopes that he is modern, to some extent suitable for the performance of services, and not altogether stupid and useless, but that is a lie, he does not only hope this, he affirms it, and he knows it. He is defiant, the untamed spirit of his ancestors is still alive in him a little, but he asks to be admonished when he acts defiantly, and, if that does not work, to be punished, for then he believes it will work. In general, it will be necessary to know how to deal with him. The undersigned believes that he is adaptable to all circumstances, therefore it is a matter of indifference to him what he is ordered to do, he is firmly convinced that any carefully executed work will be for him a greater honor than sitting idly and timidly in a cosy corner at home. A von Gunten does not sit in a cosy corner. If the ancestors of the obedient undersigned bore the knightly sword, their descendant acts in the same tradition by desiring ardently to make himself useful somehow. His modesty knows no limits, as long as one flatters his spirit, and his zeal to serve is like his ambition, which commands him to disdain obstructive and harmful feelings of honor. At home, the same undersigned always used to give his history teacher, the esteemed Dr. Merz, a drubbing, which was shameful, and which he regrets. Today he longs to be allowed to shatter his arrogance and conceit, which perhaps still animate him in part, against the merciless rock of hard work. He is reticent of speech and will never divulge confidences. He believes neither in heaven nor in hell. The satisfaction of that person who engages him will be his heaven, and the sorrowful opposite will be his annihilating hell, but he is convinced that he will give satisfaction in himself and in what he does. This firm belief gives him the courage to be the person he is,

Jacob von Gunten.

I handed the account of my life to the Principal. He read it through, I think, twice, and he seemed to like what I had written, for the shimmering ghost of a smile crossed his lips. Oh, certainly, I was watching my man very closely. He did smile a little, that is and remains a fact. At last, then, a sign of something human. What cavortings does one have to perform in order to stir people up, people whose hands one would like to kiss, even to get from them a quite fleeting friendly gesture! Intentionally, intentionally

I wrote the account of my life with such pride and cheek: "Now read it. Well? Doesn't it make you want to fling it back in my face?" Those were my thoughts. And then he gave a fine and crafty smile, this fine and crafty Principal whom I unfortunately, unfortunately revere above all others. And I noticed it. A vanguard skirmish has been won. Today I absolutely must get up to one more little piece of mischief. Or I shall die of rejoicing and laughing. But the Fräulein is crying? What is all this? Why am I so strangely happy? Am I mad?

            I must now report a matter which will perhaps raise a few doubts. And yet what I say is quite true. There is a brother of mine living in this immense city, my only brother, in my opinion an extraordinary person, his name is Johann, and he's something like a quite famous painter. I know nothing definite about his present situation in the world, since I have avoided visiting him. I shall not go to see him. If we should happen to meet on the street, and if he should recognize me and walk up to me, well and good, then I shall be pleased to give his brotherly hand a strong shake. But I shall never provoke such a meeting, never in my life. What am I, and what is he? I know what a pupil at the Benjamenta Institute is, it's obvious. Such a pupil is a good round zero, nothing more. But what my brother is at the moment I cannot know. Perhaps he's surrounded by fine, cultivated people and by God knows what formalities, and I respect formalities, therefore I don't visit my brother, for possibly a well-groomed gentleman, giving a forced smile, might come toward me. I know Johann von Gunten from earlier times, of course. He's just as cool and calculating as me and all the Guntens, but he's much older, and differences of age between people and brothers are insuperable barriers. In any case, I don't allow him to give me any pieces of good advice, and that is precisely what he will do, I fear, when he sees me, for if he sees me looking so poor and unimportant he will certainly feel provoked, as a well-situated person must, to make me feel the lowliness of my position all up and down the line, and I wouldn't be able to put up with that, I would show my von Gunten pride and become decidedly rude, for which I would later be sorry. No, a thousand times no. What? Accept charity from my brother, my own flesh and blood? I'm sorry, it's impossible. I imagine that he is very refined, smoking the world's best cigar, and lying among cushions and rugs of bourgeois snugness. And why so? Yes, there's something unbourgeois in me now, something utterly opposite to well-being, and perhaps my brother is reposing right in the midst of the loveliest, most splendid worldly well-being. It's definite: we shall not see one another, perhaps we never shall. And it isn't even necessary. Not necessary? Good, let's leave it at that. Mutton-head that I am, talking about "we" like a very dignified schoolteacher. —My brother must be surrounded, certainly, by the best and most exclusive salon behavior. Merci. Oh, thank you. Women will be there, poking their heads out at the door and asking pertly: "Now who's here again today? Oh, I say. Is he a beggar?" Thanks a lot for the welcome. I'm too kind to be pitied. Sweetly smelling flowers in the room. Oh, I don't like flowers at all. And cool cosmopolitan people? Ghastly. Yes, I'd like to see him, I'd like very much to see him. But if I saw him like this, in splendor and all snug: bang would go the feeling that this was a brother, I'd only be able to pretend happiness, and so would he. So I won't see him.

During the class, we pupils sit there, gazing rigidly to the fore, motionless. I think one isn't even allowed to blow one's personal nose. Our hands rest on our knees and are invisible during the class. Hands are the five-fingered evidence of human vanity and rapacity, therefore they stay nicely hidden under the desk. Our schoolboy noses have the greatest spiritual similarity, they all seem to strive more or less aloft, to where insight into the confusion of life floats and glows. Pupils' noses should look blunt and downcurved, that is what the rules demand, the rules which think of everything, and indeed, all our instruments of smell are humbly and meekly bent. It's as if they had been trimmed with sharp knives. Our eyes always gaze into the thoughtless emptiness, the rules demand this too. Actually one shouldn't have any eyes, for eyes are cheeky and inquisitive, and cheek and inquisitiveness are to be condemned from almost every healthy standpoint. Fairly delightful are the ears of us pupils. They hardly venture to listen, for sheer intensity of listening. They always quiver a little, as if they were frightened of being suddenly pulled in admonishment from behind, and hauled out sideways. Poor ears, having to put up with such terrors. If the sound of a call or command strikes these ears, they vibrate and tremble like harps that have been touched and disturbed. Well, now, it also happens that pupils' ears like to sleep a little, and how they are aroused! It's a joy. The best-trained part of us, though, is the mouth, it is always obediently and devoutly shut. And it's only too true: an open mouth is a yawning fact, the fact that its owner is dwelling with his few thoughts in some other place than the domain and pleasure-garden of attentiveness. A firmly shut mouth indicates open, eager ears, therefore the gates down there below the nostrils must be always carefully bolted. An open mouth is just a gob, and each of us knows that perfectly well. Lips aren't allowed to parade themselves and bloom voluptuously in the comfortable natural position, they must be folded and pressed as a sign of energetic self-denial and expectation. We pupils all do this, we treat our lips, according to the existing rules, very strictly and cruelly, and therefore we all look as grim as sergeants giving commands. A noncom wants his men, as is well known, to look as snarling and grim as he does, that suits him, for he has a sense of humor, as a rule. Seriously: people obeying usually look just like the people giving orders. A servant can't help putting on the masks and allures of his master, in order faithfully to propagate them, as it were. Now, of course, our esteemed Fräulein isn't a sergeant, on the contrary, she very often laughs, yes, she sometimes allows herself simply to laugh at us rule-obeying beaverboys, but she reckons that we shall quietly let her laugh, without changing our expressions, and that is just what we do, we act as if we didn't hear the sweet silver tones of her laughter at all. What singular oddities we are. Our hair is always neatly and smoothly combed and brushed, and everyone has to cut his own parting up there in the world on his head, a canal incised into the deep black or blond hair-earth. That's how it should be. Partings are also in the rulebook. And because we all look so charmingly barbered and parted, we all look alike, which would be a huge joke for any writer, for example, if he came on a visit to study us in our glory and littleness. This writer had better stay at home. Writers are just windbags who only want to study, make pictures and observations. To live is what matters, then the observation happens of its own accord. Our Fräulein Benjamenta would in any case let fly at such a wandering writer, blown in upon us by rain or snow, with such force that he would fall to the floor at the unfriendliness of the welcome. Then the instructress, who loves to be an autocrat, would say to us, perhaps: "Boys, help the gentleman to pick himself up." And then we pupils of the Benjamenta Institute would show the uninvited guest the whereabouts of the door. And the morsel of inquisitive authordom would disappear again. No, these are just imaginings. Our visitors are gentlemen who want to engage us boys in their service, not people with quills behind their ears.

Either the teachers in our institute do not exist, or they are still asleep, or they seem to have forgotten their profession. Or perhaps they are on strike, because nobody pays them their monthly wages? Strange feelings seize me when I think of the poor slumberers and absent minds. There they all sit, or slump, against the walls in a room specially arranged for their repose. Herr Wälchli is there, the supposed Natural History teacher. Even asleep he keeps his pipe stuck in his mouth. A pity, he would have done better as a beekeeper. How red his face still is, and how fat his oldish, softish hand. And here beside him, isn't that Herr Blösch, the much-respected French teacher? Ah, yes, it really is he, and he's telling lies when he supposes he's asleep, he's a quite terrible liar. His classes, too, consisted entirely of lies, a paper mask. How pale he looks, and how angry! He has a bad face, thick hard lips, coarse merciless features: "Are you asleep, Blösch?" He doesn't hear. He's really repulsive. And that one, who is he? Parson Strecker? Tall thin Parson Strecker, who teaches Scripture? the devil yes, it's he. "Are you asleep, Parson? All right, sleep, then, there's no harm in your sleeping. You only waste time teaching Scripture. Religion, you see, means nothing today. Sleep is more religious than all your religion. When one is asleep, one is perhaps closest to God. What do you think?" He doesn't hear. I'll go somewhere else. Ha, now who's this, choosing such a comfortable position? Is it Merz, Doctor Merz, who teaches the History of Rome? Yes, it's he, I know his pointed beard. "You seem to be angry with me Doctor Merz. Well, carry on sleeping and forget the improper scenes we had, stop scolding into your pointed beard. It's a good thing for you to sleep. For some time past, the world has been revolving around money, not around history. All the ancient heroic virtues you unpack have lost their importance long ago, you know it yourself. Thanks for some wonderful impressions. Sleep well." But here now, as I see, Herr von Bergen seems to have snuggled down, the boy-torturer von Bergen. Looks like he's dreaming, and he likes so much to bestow, with such tickling-heavenly partiality, "smacks." Or he commands: "Bend over!" and then it is such a delight for him to patch up the poor boy's backside with his meerschaum cane. A very elegant Parisian phenomenon, but cruel. And who is this here? Headmaster Wyss? Very nice. One needn't spend long on legitimate people. And who's here? Bur? Schoolmaster Bur? "I'm delighted to see you." Bur is the biggest genius of an ex-mathematics master on the continent. Only for the Benjamenta Institute he is too broad-minded and intelligent. Kraus and the others are not the right pupils for him. He is too outstanding and his demands are too high. Here in the Institute no excessive pre-conditions exist. But am I dreaming of my schoolteachers at home? In my other school there was plenty of knowledge, here there is something quite different. Something quite different to us pupils here.

Shall I get a job soon? I hope so. My photographs and my applications make, as I presume, a favorable impression. Recently I went with Schilinski to a top-class concert-café. How Schilinski trembled all over with timorousness. I behaved approximately like his kind father. The waiter ventured, after giving us a good look up and down, to ignore us; but when I requested him, with an enormously austere expression on my face, kindly to wait upon us, he at once became polite and brought us some light beer in tall, delicately cut goblets. Ah, one must play the part. A person who can throw his chest out is treated like a gentleman. One must learn to dominate situations. I know excellently well how to throw my head back, as if I were outraged by something, no, only surprised by it. I look around, as if to say: "What's this? What did you say? Is this a madhouse?" It works. I have also acquired a bearing in the Benjamenta Institute. Oh, I sometimes feel that it's within my power to play with the world and all things in it just as I please. Suddenly I understand the sweet character of women. Their coquetries amuse me and I discern profundity in their trivial gestures and manners of speaking. If one doesn't understand how it is when they raise a cup to their lips or snatch in their skirts, one will never understand them at all. Their souls go tripping along with the high-swelling heels of their sweet little boots, and their smiling is both things: a foolish habit and a piece of world history. Their conceit and their small intelligence are charming, more charming than the works of the classic authors. Often their vices are the most virtuous thing under the sun, and when they get furious and scold us? Only women know how to scold. But quiet now! I'm thinking of Mamma. How holy to me is the memory of the moments when she scolded. Quiet now, be still! What can a pupil at the Benjamenta Institute know about all these things?

I couldn't restrain myself, I've been to the office, have as usual bowed deeply, and I said to Herr Benjamenta the following words: "I have arms, legs, and hands, Herr Benjamenta, and I would like to work, and so I permit myself to ask you to obtain for me soon a job of work with pay. I know that you have all sorts of connections. To you come the most refined gentlefolk, people with crowns on their lapels of their overcoats, officers rattling sharp sabers, ladies whose robes ripple like tittering waves in their wake, older women with enormous amounts of money, old men who give a million for half a smile, people of rank, but not of intellect, people who ride about in automobiles, in a word, Principal, the world comes to you." "Now don't you be impertinent," he warned me, but, I don't know why, I no longer feel at all afraid of his fists, and I went on speaking, the words positively flew out of me: "Obtain for me at once some exciting activity. Actually my view is this: all activity is exciting. I've already learned so much from you, Principal." He said calmly: "You haven't learned anything yet." Then I took up the thread again and said: "God himself commands me to go out into life. But what is God? You are my God, Principal, if you allow me to go and earn money and respect." He was silent for a while, then he said: "Get out of this office, this instant!" That annoyed me terribly. I shouted: "In you I see an outstanding person, but I'm wrong. You're as common as the age you live in. I shall go out on the street and hold somebody up, I'm being forced to become a criminal." I knew what peril I was in. The moment I said these words I leaped for the door and then shrieked in a rage: "Adieu,

Principal!" and slid out through it, wonderfully nimbly. In the corridor I stopped and listened at the keyhole. Everything in the office was as quiet as a mouse. I went into the classroom and immersed myself in the book *What Is the Aim of the Boys' School?*

Our instruction has two sides, one theoretical and the other practical. But both sections seem to me still like a dream, like a fairy tale that is at once meaningless and rich in meaning. Learning by heart, that's one of our main tasks. I learn by heart very easily, Kraus with great difficulty, therefore he's always busy learning. The difficulties that he has to overcome are the secret of his industry, and the solution to it. He has a slow memory, and yet he impresses everything on his mind, even if it takes great effort. What he knows is then, so to speak, engraved in metal and he can never forget it again. In his case there can be no talk of forgetting. In a school where little is taught, Kraus is quite at home, therefore he's completely at home in the Benjamenta Institute. One of the maxims of our school is: "A little, but thoroughly." Well, now, Kraus stands firm on this principle, with the somewhat thick skull that is his in the world. To learn a little! The same thing over and over! Gradually I too am beginning to understand what a large world is hidden behind these words. To imprint something firmly, firmly on one's mind! I understand how important that is above all things, how good and how dignified it is. The practical or physical part of our instruction is a kind of perpetually repeated gymnastics or dancing, or whatever you want to call it. The salutation, the entrance into a room, behavior toward women or whatever, is practiced, and the practice is very long drawn out, often boring, but here too, as I now observe, and feel, there lies a deeply hidden meaning. We pupils are to be trained and shaped, as I observe, not stuffed with sciences. We are educated by being compelled to learn exactly the character of our own soul and body. We are given clearly to understand that mere discipline and sacrifice are educative, and that more blessings and more genuine knowledge are to be found in a very simple, as it were stupid, exercise than in the learning of a variety of ideas and meanings. We grasp one thing after another, and when we have grasped a thing, it is as if it possessed us. Not we possess it, but the opposite: whatever we have apparently acquired rules over us then. It is impressed upon us that a beneficent effect is to be had from acquiring a little that is firm and definite, that is to say, from growing accustomed and shaping oneself to laws and commands that prescribe a strict external discipline. Perhaps we're being stupefied, certainly we're being made small. But that doesn't make us timid, not at all. We pupils all know, one as well as the next, that timidity is a punishable offence. Whoever stutters and shows fear is exposed to the scorn of our Fräulein, but we must be small, and we must know, know precisely, that we are nothing big. The law which commands, the discipline which compels, and the many unmerciful rules which give us a direction and give us good taste: that is the big thing, not us pupils. Well, everyone feels this, even I do, that we are small, poor dependent dwarfs, obliged to be continuously obedient. And so that's how we behave: humbly, but with the utmost confidence. We are all, without exception, a little energetic, for the smallness and deprivation which are our conditions cause us to believe firmly in the few achievements that we have made. Our belief in ourselves is our modesty. If we didn't believe in anything, we wouldn't know how little we are. Nonetheless, we small young people are something. We may not be extravagant, we may not have imaginings, it is forbidden for us to look about us, and this makes us satisfied and makes us useful for any quick task. We know the world very badly, but we shall come to know it, for we shall be exposed to life and its storms. The Benjamenta school is the antechamber to the drawing rooms and palatial halls of life at large. Here we learn to feel respect, and to act as all those must act who have something to look up to. I, for one, am a little above all this, which is good, because all these impressions are so much the better for me. Precisely I have need to learn to feel esteem and respect for the objects of the world, for where would I end up if I was disrespectful to old age, if I denied God, mocked laws, and was allowed to stick my juvenile nose into everything sublime, important, and big? In my view, the present young generation is sick for precisely this reason, bellowing hell and blue murder and then miaowing for daddy and mummy when they're obliged to give in a little to duties and commandments and limitations. No, no, here the Benjamentas are my dear shining lodestars, the brother as well as the Fräulein, his sister. I will think of them as long as I live.

I have seen my brother; we met, what's more, in the thick of the city crowd. Our meeting turned out to be a very friendly one. It was unforced and affectionate. Johann behaved very nicely, and probably I did, too. We went to a small, reticent restaurant and had a talk there. "Just you go on being yourself, brother," Johann said to me, "begin from all the way down, that's fine. If you need help . . ." I made a gesture of refusal. He went on: "For look, you see, it's hardly worth it, up there at the top. If you see what I mean. Don't misunderstand me, brother." I gave a lively nod, for I knew in advance what he was saying, but I asked him to go on, and he said: "It's the atmosphere up there. I mean, they've all got an air of having done enough, and that stops things, it's cramping. I hope you don't quite understand me, for, if you did understand me, brother, you'd be a dreadful person." We laughed. Oh, to be able to laugh with my brother, I like that. He said: "You are now, so to speak, a zero, my good brother. But when one is young, one should be a zero, for nothing is more ruinous than being a bit important early on, too early on. Certainly: you're a bit important to yourself. That's fine. Excellent. But for the world you're still nothing, and that's almost just as excellent. I keep hoping you won't quite understand me, for if you understood me completely . . ." "I'd be a dreadful person," I broke in. We laughed again. It was very jolly. A strange fire began to animate me. My eyes were burning. I like it very much, by the way, when I feel so burned up. My face gets quite red. And then thoughts full of purity and loftiness usually assail me. Johann went on, he said: "Brother, please, don't always interrupt me. That silly young laughter of yours has a stifling effect on ideas. Listen! Pay close attention now. What I'm telling you may be useful to you one day. Above all: never think of yourself as an outcast. There are no outcasts, brother, for perhaps there's nothing in this world that's worth aspiring to. And yet you must aspire, even passionately so. But so as to become not too full of longings: realize that there is nothing, nothing worth aspiring to. Everything is rotten. Do you understand that? Look, I keep hoping that you can't quite understand all this. It worries me." I said: "Unfortunately I'm too intelligent to misunderstand you, as you hope I might. But don't worry. Your revelations don't frighten me at all." We smiled at one another. Then we ordered some more drinks, and Johann, who, by the way, did look uncommonly ele-

gant, went on talking: "Of course there's progress on earth, so
called, but that's only one of the many lies which the business
people put out, so that they can squeeze money out of the crowd
more blatantly and mercilessly. The masses are the slaves of today,
and the individual is the slave of the vast mass-ideas. There's
nothing beautiful and excellent left. You must dream up beauty
and goodness and justice. Tell me, do you know how to dream?"
I contented myself with a nod, two nods, and let Johann carry
on while I listened intently: "Try to earn lots and lots of money.
Everything else has gone wrong, but not money. Everything, everything is spoiled, halved, robbed of grace and splendor. Our cities
are vanishing relentlessly from the face of the earth. Big chunks
of nothing are taking up the space once occupied by dwellings
and princely palaces. The piano, dear brother, and the tinkling
that goes with it. Concerts and theaters are going down and down,
the standpoint sinks lower and lower. There is, to be sure, still
something like a society that sets the tone, but it no longer has the
capacity for striking the notes of dignity and subtlety of mind.
There are books—in a word, don't ever despair. Keep on being
poor and despised, dear friend. Give up the money-idea, too. It's
the most lovely and triumphant thing, it makes one a very poor
devil. Rich people, Jakob, are very unsatisfied and unhappy. The
rich today: they've got nothing left. They are the really starving
people." I nodded again. It's true, I say yes to everything very
easily. But I liked what Johann said, and it suited me. There was
pride in what he said, and sorrow. And, well, these two together,
pride and sorrow, have a good sound. We ordered some more beer
and my opposite number said: "You must hope and yet hope for
nothing. Look up to something, yes, do that, because that is right
for you, you're young, terribly young, Jakob, but always admit to

yourself that you despise it, the thing that you're looking up to with respect. Nodding again, are you? Lord, what an intelligent listener you are. You're like a tree hung with understanding. Be content, dear brother, strive, learn, do whatever good and kind things you can for people. Look, I've got to go. When shall we meet again? Frankly, you interest me—" We went out and on the street we said goodbye. For a long time I watched my dear brother as he walked away. Yes, he's my brother. How glad I am that he is.

My father has a coach and horses and a servant, old Fehlmann. Mamma has her own box at the theater. How she is envied by the women of the town, with its 28,000 inhabitants! Despite her age, my mother is still a pretty woman, even a beautiful one. I remember a light-blue, tightly fitting dress that she once wore. She was holding up a delicately white sunshade. The sun was shining. It was splendid Spring weather. In the streets there was a smell of violets. People were out for a stroll and beneath the green foliage of the trees in the park the band was playing. How sweet and bright everything was! A fountain was splashing, and children in light-colored clothes were laughing and playing. And a soft caressing breeze was blowing, with fragrances in it, awakening desire for inexpressible things. From the windows of houses on the Neuquartierplatz people were looking out. Mother was wearing long pale-yellow gloves over her slender hands and sweet arms. Johann had at that time already left home. But father was there. No, never shall I accept help (money) from the parents whom I so tenderly respect. My injured pride would fling me onto a sickbed and bang would go all my dreams of an independent life, destroyed forever these ardently cherished plans for self-education. That's the point: to educate myself, or prepare myself for a future education, that is why I became a pupil at the Benjamenta Institute, for here one readies oneself for some darkly approaching arduous task. And that is also why I don't write home, for even writing about it would make me have doubts about myself, would completely ruin my plan for starting from all the way down. Something great and audacious must happen in secrecy and silence, or it perishes and falls away, and the fire that was awakened dies again. I know how I want it, that's enough. —Ah, yes, that was it. I have a merry tale in store, about our old servant Fehlmann, who is still alive and in service. It was like this: Fehlmann did something very wrong one day and he was going to be dismissed. "Fehlmann," said Mamma, "you can go. We do not need you any more." Thereupon the poor old man, who shortly before this had buried a son of his who had died of cancer (that isn't funny), threw himself at my mother's feet and begged for mercy, yes, actually for mercy. The poor devil, he had tears in his old eyes. Mamma forgives him. I recount the scene next day to my friends, the Weibel brothers, and they laugh me to scorn. They stop being my friends, because they think that my family is too royalistic. They find this falling at someone's feet suspicious, and they go along and slander me and Mamma in the most tasteless way. Like regular little boys, yes, but also like regular little republicans, for whom the dispensing of personal and autocratic mercy or displeasure is a monstrosity and an object of revulsion. How comical it seems to me now! And yet how significant this small incident is for the tendency of the times. The whole world today judges as the Weibel brothers did. Yes, that's how it is: nothing lordly or ladylike is tolerated any more. There are no more masters who can do as they please, and there haven't been any mistresses for ages. Should I be sad about this? It wouldn't even cross my mind. Am I responsible for the spirit of the age? I take the times as they come and only reserve the right to make my own quiet observations. Good old Fehlmann: he was pardoned, in the patriarchal way. Tears of loyalty and dependence, how beautiful that is!

From three o'clock in the afternoon we pupils are left almost completely to our own devices. Nobody bothers with us any more. The Benjamentas are secluded in the inner chambers and in the classroom there's an emptiness, an emptiness that almost sickens one. All noise is forbidden. One is only allowed to scurry and creep about and to talk in whispers. Schilinski looks at himself in his mirror, Schacht looks out of the window or he gesticulates to the kitchen maids on the other side of the street, and Kraus is learning things by heart, murmuring the lessons to himself. It's as quiet as the grave. The courtyard out there lies deserted, like a foursquare eternity, and I usually practice standing on one leg. Often, for a change, I see how long I can hold my breath. That is an exercise, too, and it is even supposed to be good for the health, as a doctor once told me. Or I write. Or I close my untired eyes, so as to see nothing any more. The eyes transmit thoughts, therefore I shut them from time to time, in order to stop having to think. When one is just there like this and doing nothing, one suddenly feels how painful existence can be. To do nothing and yet maintain one's bearing, that requires energy, a person doing something has an easy time in comparison. We pupils are masters of this kind of propriety. Ordinarily, do-nothings start something out of boredom, lounge about, fidget, yawn broadly or sigh. We pupils do nothing like this. We close

our lips firmly and are motionless. Over our heads the grumpy
rules are always floating. Sometimes, when we are sitting or standing there, the door opens and the Fräulein walks slowly through
the schoolroom, giving us a strange look. She always seems like a
ghost to me. It's as if it were someone coming from far far away.
"What are you doing, boys?" she may ask then, but she doesn't
wait for an answer, she walks on. How beautiful she is! What a
luxuriance of raven hair! Mostly one sees her with her eyes downcast. She has eyes that are wonderfully apt for being downcast.
Her eyelids (oh, I observe all these things very sharply) are richly
curved and are curiously capable of quick movement. These eyes!
If one ever sees them, one looks down into something frighteningly
abyssal and profound. These eyes, with their shining darkness,
seem to say nothing and yet to say everything unspeakable, they
are so familiar and yet so unknown. The eyebrows are thin to
breaking and are drawn in rounded arches over the eyes. If you
look at them, you have a prickly feeling. They are like crescent
moons in a morbidly pallid evening sky, like fine wounds, but all
the more sharp, inwardly cutting wounds. And her cheeks! Silent
yearning and swooning seem to celebrate festivities on them. There
is a weeping on them, up and down, of delicacy and tenderness
that nobody has understood. Sometimes there appears on the
shimmering snow of these cheeks a soft imploring red, a reddish
timid life, a sun, no, not that, only the faint reflection of such a
sun. Then it's as if the cheeks were suddenly smiling, or a little
feverish. When one looks at Fräulein Benjamenta's cheeks, one
has no more joy in living, for one has the feeling that life must
be a turbulent hell full of vile crudities. Such delicacy as this almost forces one to look deep into such hardness and peril. And
her teeth, which one sees shimmering when she parts her full and

kindly lips in a smile. And when she weeps. One thinks that the earth must drop away from every footfall of hers, in shame and sorrow to be seeing her weep. And when one only hears her weeping? Oh, then one swoons away. Recently we heard her, right there in the schoolroom. We were all trembling like aspens. Yes, all of us, we love her. She is our instructress, our higher being. And something is making her suffer, that is obvious. Is she unwell?

Fräulein Benjamenta has spoken a few words with me, in the kitchen. I was just going up to my room, and she asked me, without honoring me with a look: "How are you getting on, Jakob? Is everything all right?" I at once stood at attention, as is required, and said in a submissive voice: "Oh, yes, certainly, Fräulein Benjamenta. Things just couldn't go wrong for me." She smiled faintly and asked: "What does that mean?" She said it over her shoulder. I replied: "I have everything I need." She looked at me for a moment and was silent. After a while she said: "You can go, Jakob. You're excused now. You needn't stand there." I did her the honor prescribed, bowing, and rushed to my room. Hardly five minutes had passed when there was a knock. I leaped to the door. I knew the knock. She stood there before me. "Jakob," she said, "tell me, how do you get on with the other boys? They're nice people, don't you find?" My answer was that I felt I liked and respected them all, without exception. The instructress looked at me cunningly, with her beautiful eyes, and said: "Well, well. And yet you do quarrel with Kraus. Is quarreling for you a sign of love and respect?" I replied without hesitating: "Yes, to some extent, Fräulein. This quarreling isn't meant so seriously, you see. If Kraus were clever, he would notice that I like him better than any of the others. I respect Kraus very very much. It would hurt me to think that you didn't believe that." She took my hand and pressed it lightly and said: "All right, now, don't get excited. You must watch out, when you get heated. You hothead. If things are as you say, then I must be content with you. I shall be content, too, if you go on being well-behaved. Yes, remember this: Kraus is a splendid boy and it offends me when you don't behave well with him. Be nice to him. That is my special wish. But don't be sad, now. Look, I'm not reproaching you. What a coddled and pampered little aristocrat you are! Kraus is such a good person. Isn't it so, isn't Kraus a good person, Jakob?" I said: "Yes." Nothing more than Yes and then suddenly I couldn't help giving a rather stupid laugh, I don't know why. She shook her head and went away. Why did I have to laugh? I still don't know. But it's not a matter of any importance. When shall I get some money? This question seems important. Money, as I see it, has a completely ideal value at the moment. When I imagine the clink of a gold coin, I go practically frantic. I have food to eat: so what. I would like to be rich and smash my head in. Soon I shan't like eating any more.

If I were rich, I wouldn't travel around the world. To be sure, that would not be so bad. But I can see nothing wildly exciting about getting a fugitive acquaintance with foreign places. In general I would decline to educate myself, as they say, any further. I would be attracted by deep things and by the soul, rather than by distances and things far off. It would fascinate me to investigate what is near at hand. And I wouldn't buy anything, either. I would make no acquisitions. Elegant clothes, fine underwear, a top hat, modest gold cufflinks, long patent leather shoes, that would be about all, and with these things I would start out.

No house, no garden, no servant, yes, a servant, I would engage a good, dignified Kraus. And then I could begin. Then I would walk out into the swirling mist on the street. Winter with its melancholy cold would match my gold coins excellently. I would carry the banknotes in a simple briefcase. I would walk about on foot, just as usual, with the consciously secret intention of not letting people notice very much how regally rich I am. Perhaps, too, it would be snowing. All the same to me, on the contrary, that would suit me fine. Soft snowfall among the evening glow of street-lamps. It would be glittering, fascinating. It would never occur to me to take a cab. Only people who are in a hurry or want to put on noble airs do that. But I wouldn't want to put on noble airs, and I would be in no hurry whatever. Thoughts would occur to me as I strolled along. Suddenly I would greet someone, very politely, and look, it's a man. Very politely, then, I would look at the man, then I would see that he's having hard times. I would notice this, not see it, one notices such things, even if one hardly sees them, but there's something about it that one sees. Well, now, anyway, this man would ask me what I want, and his question would be a cultivated one. This question would be asked very gently and simply, and I would be very deeply moved by it. For I would have been quite expecting something harsh. "This man must have been deeply wounded," I would at once say to myself, "otherwise he would have got annoyed." And then I would say nothing, absolutely nothing, but it would be enough to keep looking at him, more and more. Not a sharp look, no, a very simple look, perhaps even rather a blithe one. And then I would know who he was. I would open my briefcase, would extract from it ten thousand marks in ten separate notes, and would give this sum to the man. Then I would doff my hat, as politely as ever, say goodnight, and walk away. And it would go on snowing. As I walked along I would not be thinking any more thoughts, I wouldn't be able to, I would be feeling far too good for anything like that. The man was a horribly destitute artist, I knew it for certain, it was to him that I had given the money. Yes, I knew it, for I wouldn't have let myself be deceived. Oh, there would be one great passionate worry less in the world. Well, now, the next night I would perhaps have some quite different ideas. In any case I wouldn't travel around the world, but would prefer to get up to some crazy and foolish tricks. For example, I could give a madly rich and joyous banquet and arrange orgies such as the world has never seen. I would like it to cost one hundred thousand marks. Quite definitely the money would have to be spent in an utterly wild way, for only genuinely wasted money would be— would have been—beautiful money. And one day I would be a beggar and the sun would be shining and I would be so happy, and I wouldn't ever want to know why. And then Mamma would come and hug me—what nice imaginings these are!

Kraus's face and nature have something old about them, and this oldness he radiates takes anyone who looks at him away to Palestine. The times of Abraham come to life again in the face of my fellow-pupil. The old patriarchal epoch, with its mysterious customs and landscapes, rises to the surface and gazes at one paternally. I feel as if all people in that time were fathers with ancient faces and long brown complicated beards, which is nonsense, of course, and yet perhaps there is something in this very simple-minded notion that corresponds to facts. Yes, in that time! Even this phrase, "in that time": how parental and domestic it sounds! In the old Israelite time there could very well be, now and again, a Papa Isaac or Abraham, he enjoyed respect and lived out the days of his old age in natural wealth, which consisted in landed property. In those days something like majesty surrounded grey old age. Old men were in those days like kings, and the years they had lived meant the same as the same number of acquired titles of nobility. And how young these old men kept! They were still begetting sons and daughters at the age of a hundred. In those days there were still no dentists, so one must assume that there were absolutely no decayed teeth either. And how beautiful, for example, Joseph in Egypt is. Kraus has about him something of Joseph in Potiphar's house. He has been sold into the house as a young slave, and look, they are bringing him into the presence of an immensely rich, honest, and fine man. There he is now, a household slave, but he has a pleasant time of it. The laws in those days were perhaps inhuman, certainly, but the customs and usages and ideas were correspondingly more delicate and refined. Today a slave would have a much harder time, God help him. Of course, too, there are very very many slaves in the midst of us arrogantly ready-made modern people. Perhaps all we present-day people are something like slaves, ruled by an angry, whip-wielding, unrefined idea of the world. —Well and good, now one day the lady of the house demands of Joseph that he do what she desires. How peculiar that such backstairs stories are still very well known today, they live on, from mouth to mouth, through all ages. In all primary schools the story is taught, and do people still object to Joseph's pedantry? I despise people who underestimate the beauty of pedantry, they are thoroughly mindless people, weak in judgment. Good, and then Kraus, I mean Joseph, refuses. But it could very well be Kraus, because there is something very like Joseph in Egypt about him. "No, my lady, I wouldn't do a thing like that, I owe loyalty to my liege lord." Then the lady, who is, incidentally, charming, goes and accuses the young servant of committing a base deed and of trying to seduce his lady into an error. But I don't know any more. Peculiar that I don't know what Potiphar said and did next. I can still see the Nile quite clearly. Yes, Kraus could be Joseph, or anything, for that matter. His bearing, figure, face, haircut, and gestures are incomparably suitable. Even his unfortunately still-uncured skin feature. Spots are Biblical, oriental. And his morality, character, the firm possession of a chaste young man's virtues? They are wonderfully suitable. Joseph in Egypt, too, must be a good all-around little pedant, or else he would have obeyed the wanton woman and have been disloyal to his lord. Kraus would act precisely as his ancient Egyptian likeness did. He would raise his hands in protest, and say with a half-imploring, half-chastising look on his face: "No, no, I wouldn't do a thing like that," et cetera.

Dear Kraus! My thoughts keep returning to him. In him one can see what the word "culture" really means. Later in life, wherever he goes, Kraus will be regarded as a useful but uncultivated person, but for me he is thoroughly cultivated, and mainly because he is the embodiment of good, steadfast wholeness. One can even call him a culture in human form. Around Kraus there are no flutterings of winged and whispered knowledge, but something in him is at rest, and he himself, he rests and reposes on something. One can safely entrust one's very soul to his keeping. He will never deceive or slander anybody, and, well, this above all, this non-talkativeness, that's what I call culture. Anyone who chatters is a deceiver, he may be a very nice person, but this talking about everything that enters his head makes him a common fellow and a bad one. Kraus is guarded, he always keeps something back, he thinks that it is unnecessary just to talk, and this has the same effect as goodness and a lively leniency. That's what I call culture. Kraus is unkind and often fairly rough to people of his own age and sex, and precisely this is why I like him, for it proves to me that he would be incapable of brutal and thoughtless betrayal. He is loyal and decent to everybody. For that's the trouble: out of common kindness one usually just goes along and desecrates in the most terrible way the reputations and lives of neighbors, friends, even brothers. Kraus doesn't know much, but he is never, never thoughtless, he always subjects himself to certain commands of his own making, and that's what I call culture. Whatever is kind and thoughtful about a person is culture. And there's so much else besides. To be so far removed from any and every self-seeking, even in a small way, and to be so close to self-discipline as Kraus, that is what I think made Fräulein Benjamenta say: "Isn't it so, Jakob, Kraus is good?" Yes, he's good. When I lose this friend, I lose a kingdom of heaven, I know it. And I'm almost afraid to quarrel freely with Kraus. I only want to contemplate him, always to contemplate him, for later I shall have to content myself with his image, because rampageous life is certain to separate the two of us.

I now understand also why Kraus has no outward advantages, no physical graces, why nature has so dwarfishly squashed and disfigured him. She wants something from him, she has plans for him, or she had plans for him from the start. Perhaps this person was, for nature, too pure, and that's why she threw him into an insignificant, small, unbeautiful body, in order to preserve him against pernicious outward successes. Or perhaps it wasn't so, and nature was annoyed and malicious when she made Kraus. But how sorry she must be now, to have treated him like a wicked stepmother! And who knows. Perhaps she rejoices in this graceless masterpiece of hers, and indeed she would have cause to rejoice, for this graceless Kraus is more beautiful than the most graceful and beautiful people. He doesn't shine with talents, but with the radiance of a good and unspoiled heart, and his plain bad manners, despite the woodenness attaching to them, are perhaps the most beautiful kind of motion and manners that there can be in human society. No, Kraus will never have any successes, either with women, who will find him dry and ugly, or otherwise in the world, which will pass him heedlessly by. Heedlessly? Yes, nobody will ever pay any attention to Kraus, and precisely this, his going on living without enjoying attention, that is the wonderful thing, which seems to be part of a plan, the sign of the Creator. God gives a Kraus to this world, in order to entrust to it, as it were, a deep, insoluble riddle. And the riddle will never be understood, for look: people don't even try to solve it, and for this very reason the Kraus riddle is such a glorious and deep one: because nobody wants to solve it, because there isn't a person living who'll suppose there is some task, some riddle, or a more delicate meaning, at the back of this nameless, inconspicuous Kraus. Kraus is a genuine work of God, a nothing, a servant. To everyone he will seem uncultivated, just about good enough to do the roughest work, and it is strange: people won't be wrong in this either, but they'll be perfectly right, for it is true: Kraus, modesty itself, the crown, the palace of humility, he will do menial work, he can do it and he will do it. He has no thought but to help, to obey and to serve, and people will at once notice and exploit this, and in this exploiting of him lies such a radiant, golden, divine justice, shimmering with goodness and splendor. Yes, Kraus is the image of legitimate being, utterly monotonous, monosyllabic, and unambiguous being. Nobody will mistake this person's plainness, and therefore nobody will notice him, and he will be thoroughly unsuccessful. Charming, charming, three times charming I find this. Oh, the creations of God are so full of grace, of charm, beribboned with charms and thoughts. People will think that this is a very excessive way of putting it. Well, I must confess it's not by any means the most excessive thing. No, for Kraus no success will ever flower, no fame, no love, that is very good, for successes go inseparably with fickleness and a few cheap ideas about life. One notices it at once, when people have successes and recognition to display, they grow fat with satiating complacency, and the power of vanity blows them up like balloons, so that they become unrecognizable. God preserve a good person from being recognized by the crowd. If it doesn't make him bad, it merely confuses and weakens him. Gratitude, yes. Gratitude is something quite different. But nobody will ever be grateful to Kraus, and that too isn't necessary. Once every ten years somebody will perhaps say to Kraus: "Thanks, Kraus," and then give a stupid, cruelly stupid smile. My Kraus will never go to ruin, because there will always be great and loveless difficulties confronting him. I think that I, I am one of the very few people, perhaps the only person, or perhaps there are two or three, who will know what they have in Kraus, or have had in him. The Fräulein, yes, she knows. Also the Principal, perhaps. Yes, certainly he knows. Herr Benjamenta is certainly penetrating enough to know what Kraus is worth. I must stop writing for today. It excites me too much. I'm getting confused. And the letters are flickering and dancing in front of my eyes.

Behind our house there is an old, neglected garden. When I see it in the early morning from the office window (every other morning I have to tidy the office, together with Kraus), I am sorry for it, lying there untended, and each time I want to go down and look after it. But those are sentimental ideas. The devil take such misleading dreamy softness. There are quite other gardens with us in the Benjamenta Institute. To go into the real garden is forbidden. No pupils are allowed in there. I don't really know why. But, as I said, we have another garden, perhaps more beautiful than the actual one. In our primer, *What Is the Aim of the Boys' School?*, it says on page 8: "Good behavior is a garden full of flowers." It's in such gardens of spirit and sentiment that we pupils are allowed to leap around. Not bad. If one of us is badly behaved, he walks of his own accord in a horrible dark hell. If he is good, he can't help going out for his reward among shady green leaves flecked with sunlight. How seductive! And in my poor boyish opinion, there is some truth in that nice dogma. If a person behaves stupidly, he must be ashamed and angry with himself, and that is the painful hell in which he sweats. But if he has been attentive and compliant, then something invisible takes him by the hand, something friendly, like a little spirit, and that is the garden, the kind dispensation, and then he really does go strolling of his own accord over friendly green meadows. If ever a pupil at the Benjamenta Institute is allowed to be satisfied with himself, which seldom occurs, since the rules are always storming at us, with hail, snow, lightning, and rain, then there is a fragrance all around him, and it is the sweet fragrance of modest but staunchly fought-for praise. If Fräulein Benjamenta utters a word of praise, the fragrance comes, and if she scolds, then the schoolroom goes dark. What a peculiar world, our school. If a pupil has been well behaved and seemly, there is suddenly a vault overhead, and it is the blue irreplaceable heaven above the imaginary garden. If we pupils have been very patient, and if we have maintained our exertions well, if we have been able, as they say, to stand and wait, then suddenly before our somewhat weary eyes the air turns gold, and we know that it is the heavenly sun. Anyone with a right and title to fatigue finds the sun shining down upon him. And if there has been no need for us to catch ourselves having impure wishes, which always make one so unhappy, then we listen and, aha! what is that? Birds are singing! Well, it must have been the happy and fine-feathered songsters of our garden who were singing and making their graceful clamor. Now admit: do we pupils of the Benjamenta Institute need any other gardens than those which we create for ourselves? We are rich lords, if we conduct ourselves with delicacy and good manners. Whenever, for example, I wish to possess money, which unfortunately is all too often the case, then I sink into the deep gulfs of hopeless, raging desire, oh, then I suffer and swoon, and doubt if I shall ever be rescued. And then, if I look at Kraus, a deep, murmuring, springlike, wonderful comfort takes hold of me. That is the peaceful spring of modesty, which rises in our garden, splashing up and down, and then I am so happy, in such a good mood, so attuned to goodness. Ah, and they say I don't love Kraus? If one of us is, that is to say, were to have been, a hero, if he had done something brave in peril of his life (that's what it says in the primer), then he would be allowed to enter the pillared marble house with its wall paintings that is hidden among the greenery of our garden, and there a mouth would kiss him. The primer doesn't say what sort of a mouth. And of course we aren't heroes.

And why should we be? First, we have no chance to behave like heroes, and second: I doubt if Schilinski, for example, or Beanpole Peter, could be inveigled into making sacrifices. Even without kisses, heroes, and pillared pavilions, our garden is a nice arrangement, I think. Talking of heroes gives me the shivers. I'd rather not say anything on that.

Recently I asked Kraus if he too didn't sometimes feel something like boredom. He gave me a reproving and corrective look, thought for a moment, and said: "Boredom? That's not very clever of you, Jakob. And, let me tell you, your questions are as naive as they are sinful. Whoever can be bored in this world? You, perhaps. Not me, I can tell you. I'm learning things by heart from this book here. Well? Have I got time to be bored? What foolish questions. Noble folk get bored, perhaps, not Kraus, and you get bored, or you wouldn't think of the idea, and wouldn't come to me asking such a thing. One can always be doing something, if not outside, then at least inside, one can murmur, Jakob. I know you've often laughed at me on account of my murmuring, but listen and tell me, do you know what I murmur? Words, Jakob. I always murmur and repeat words. It does one good, I can tell you. Get away with you and your boredom. People who get bored are ones who always reckon that something amusing ought to come at them from outside. Boredom is where bad moods are, and where people want things. Go away now, don't bother me, let me learn, go away and do some work. Bother yourself with something, then you certainly won't feel bored any more. And in the future please avoid such almost exasperating, utterly silly questions." I asked: "Is that all you had to say, Kraus?" and laughed. But he just looked at me pityingly. No, Kraus can never be bored, never. I knew that perfectly well, I only wanted to tease him again. How nasty of me that is, and how empty headed. I definitely must improve. How bad it is, always to be wanting to ape and annoy Kraus! And yet: how delightful! His reproaches sound so funny. There is something of old father Abraham in his admonitions.

What a terrible dream I had a few days ago. In the dream I had become a very bad man indeed. I couldn't make out how. I was crude, from top to toe, a dressed-up, crass, and cruel bit of human flesh. I was fat, things were going splendidly for me, it seemed. Rings glittered on the fingers of my coarse hands, and I had a belly with flabby hundredweights of fleshy dignity hanging down it. I felt so completely that I could give commands and let fly with moods. Beside me, on a table richly spread, shone the objects of an insatiable appetite for food and drink, bottles of wine and liqueurs, and the most exquisite cold dishes. I had only to reach out a hand, and from time to time I did so. To the knives and forks clung the tears of enemies I destroyed, and the glasses sang with the sighs of many poor people, but the tear-stains only made me want to laugh, while the hopeless sighs sounded to me like music. I needed banquet music and had it. Evidently I had been extremely successful in business at the expense of the well-being of others, and that put joy into my very guts. Oh, oh, how I reveled in the knowledge of having pulled the ground from under the feet of a few fellow-men! And I reached for the bell and rang. An old man walked in, no, excuse me, crawled in, it was Wisdom, and the fellow crawled up to my boots, to kiss them. And I let him do this, in his humiliation. Just think: experience itself, the good and noble precept: it kissed my feet. That's what I call being rich. Because I felt like it, I rang again, for I had an itch, I don't recall where it was, for an ingenious change, and in came a young girl, a real delicacy for a libertine like me. Childish Innocence, that's what she called herself, and she began with a glance at the whip at my side, to kiss me, which was incredibly refreshing. Fear and her precocious depravity fluttered in the child's beautiful deer-like eyes. When I had had enough of her, I rang again and in came Seriousness, a handsome, slim, but poor young man. He was one of my lackeys, and I ordered him, with a scowl, to fetch that thingummy, what's its name, can't remember, now I've got it, Joy-in-Work. Soon after this, in came Zeal and I took the pleasure of giving him, the complete man, this splendidly built Working Man, a lash with the whip, right in the middle of his quietly waiting face, it was a tremendous laugh. And he didn't mind, native creative energy himself, he didn't mind. Then, of course, with an indolent condescending gesture I invited him to have a glass of wine, and the foolish idiot drank up this wine of his disgrace. "Off you go now, work for me," I said, and he left. Then Virtue came in, a female figure of overwhelming beauty for anyone not frozen rigid, and weeping. I took her on my knee and fooled around with her. When I had robbed her of her unspeakable treasure, the Ideal, I chased her out with derision, and then I whistled and God himself appeared. I shouted: "What? You too?" And I woke up, dripping with sweat—how glad I was that it was only a bad dream. My God, I do hope that I shall make something of myself one day. How close to the edge of madness everything is in dreams! Kraus would goggle at me like anything if I were to tell him all this.

The way we revere the Fräulein really is comic. But I, for one, am all in favor of comedy, it certainly has its magic. The class always begins at eight. But we pupils sit there for ten minutes beforehand, in our seats, full of excitement and expectation, and we gaze fixedly at the door through which the Principaless will appear. For this kind of anticipatory display of respect, we also have exact rules. It's as good as law that we should listen for her, to tell when she is coming, she who will certainly enter at a particular time. For ten silly-boy-like minutes, we pupils have to be getting ready to stand up in our places. All these petty requirements are slightly humiliating, actually they're ridiculous, but it's a question not of our personal honor but of the honor of the Benjamenta Institute, and that is possibly just as it should be, for does the pupil have any honor at all? Not a scrap. To be well and truly regimented and harrassed, that's the highest of honors for us. To be drilled is an honor for pupils, that's as clear as day. But we don't rebel, either. It would never cross our minds. We have, collectively, so few thoughts. I have perhaps the most thoughts, that's quite possible, but at root I despise my capacity for thinking. I value only experiences, and these, as a rule, are quite independent of all thinking and comparing. Thus I value the way in which I open a door. There is more hidden life in opening a door than in asking a question. Yet everything does provoke one to question and compare and remember. Certainly one must think, one must even think a great deal. But to comply, that is much more refined, much more than thinking. If one thinks, one resists, and that is always so ugly and ruinous to things. Thinkers, if only they knew what harm they do. Anyone who industriously does not think, does something, he certainly does, and that is more neces-

sary. There are ten thousand superfluous heads at work in the
world. It's clear, clear as day. The generations of men are losing
the joy of life with all their treatises and understandings and knowledge. If, for example, a pupil of the Benjamenta Institute doesn't
know that he's being polite, then polite is what he's being. If he
knows it, then all his unconscious grace and politeness disappear,
and he makes some mistake or other. I like running down stairs.
What a lot of talk!

It's nice to be a bit prosperous and to have
one's worldly affairs somewhat in order. I've been to my brother
Johann's apartment, and I must say it was a pleasant surprise,
it's quite an old-fashioned von Guntenish place. The mere fact
that the floor is covered with a soft, dull-blue carpet, I found ex-
traordinarily imposing. All the rooms show taste, not ostentatious
taste, but a definite and fine choiceness. The furniture is placed
gracefully, which has the effect of greeting you politely and gently
when you come in. There are mirrors on the walls. There's even
one big mirror that reaches from floor to ceiling. The particular
objects are old, yet not old, elegant, yet not elegant. There's
warmth and carefulness in the rooms, one feels this, and it's pleasant. A free and solicitous will hung the mirrors up and showed
the delicately curved sofa to its place. I wouldn't be a von Gunten
if I didn't notice that. Everything is clean and without dust, and
yet it doesn't all shine, but everything looks at one calmly and
serenely. Nothing strikes the eye sharply. The whole combination
has a significant kindly look. A beautiful black cat was lying on
the dark red plush chair, like black, soft easefulness bedded in red.
Very pretty. If I were a painter, I'd paint the intimacy of such an
animal image. My brother came toward me in a very friendly way

and we stood facing one another like measured men of the world
who know how enjoyable the proprieties can be. We talked of this
and that. Then a large and slender snow-white dog ran up to us,
with graceful joyous movements. Well, naturally I stroked the
animal. Everything about Johann's apartment is good. He took
the trouble to discover, with love, each of the objects and pieces
of furniture in antique shops, until he had collected together the
cosiest and most graceful ones. He has managed to make something simple but perfect within modest limits, so that convenient
and useful objects join with beautiful and graceful ones and make
his apartment look like a painting. Soon, as we sat there, a young
lady appeared and Johann introduced me to her. Later, we drank
tea and were very happy. The cat miaowed for milk and the beautiful large dog wanted to eat some of the biscuits that were on
the table. Both animals also had their wishes gratified. Evening
came and I had to go home.

Here in the Benjamenta Institute one learns to
suffer and endure losses, and that is in my view a craft, an exercise
without which any person will always remain a big child, a sort
of crybaby, however important he may be. We pupils have no
hopes, it is even forbidden to us to nourish hopes for life in our
hearts, and yet we are completely calm and happy. How can that
be? Do we feel that guardian angels, or something similar, are
flying back and forth over our smoothly combed heads? I can't
say. Perhaps we are happy and carefree from being so restricted.
That's quite possible. But does that make the happiness and fresh-
ness of our hearts any less valuable? Are we really stupid? We
have our vibrations. Unconsciously or consciously we take thought
for many things, we are with the spirits here and there, and we

send out our feelings in all directions, gathering experiences and observations. There's so much that comforts us, because we are, in general, very zealous and inquiring people, and because we set little value on ourselves. A person who sets a high value on himself is never safe from discouragements and humiliations, for confronting a self-conscious person there is always something hostile to consciousness. And yet we pupils aren't by any means without dignity, but the dignity we have is a very very mobile, small, pliant, and supple dignity. Also we put it on and off, according to the requirements. Are we products of a higher culture, or are we nature-boys? I don't know that either. One thing I do know for certain: we are waiting! That's our value. Yes, we're waiting, and we are, as it were, listening to life, listening out into that plateau which people call the world, out across the sea with its storms. Fuchs, by the way, has left. I was very glad of that. I couldn't get along with him.

       I have spoken with Herr Benjamenta, that's to say, he has spoken with me. "Jakob," he said to me, "tell me, don't you find the life here sterile, sterile? Eh? I'd like to know your opinion. Be quite frank with me." I preferred not to say anything, but not out of defiance. My defiance disappeared long ago. But I said nothing, and roughly in such a way that my answer would have been: "Sir, allow me not to say anything. In reply to such a question, the most I could say would be something unseemly." Herr Benjamenta looked at me closely, and I thought he understood my silence. And it really was so, for he smiled and said: "You're wondering, aren't you, Jakob, why I spend my life here in the Institute so lethargically, so absent-mindedly, as it were? Isn't that so? Have you noticed it? But the last thing I want is

to lead you astray into giving outrageous answers. I must confess
something to you, Jakob. Listen, I think you're an intelligent and
decent young person. Now, please, be cheeky. And I feel that I
must confess something else to you: I, your Principal, think well
of you. And a third confession: I have begun to feel a strange,
a quite peculiar and now no longer repressible preference for you.
You'll be cheeky with me now, won't you, Jakob? You will, won't
you?—now that I've revealed something of myself to you, young
man, you'll dare to treat me with disdain? And you'll defy me
now? Is it so, tell me, is it so?" We two, the bearded man and I,
the boy, looked one another in the eye. It was like an inner combat.
I was about to open my mouth and say something submissive,
but I managed to control myself and said nothing. And now I
noticed that the Principal, this gigantic man, was trembling slightly. From this moment, some common bond was between us. I felt
it, yes, I didn't only feel it, I knew it. "Herr Benjamenta respects
me," I told myself, and as a result of this realization, which came
down on me like a flash of lightning, I found it right, even im-
perative, not to say anything. All the worse for me if I had said
a single word. A single word would have made me into an insignificant little pupil again, and I had just risen to the most
unpupil-like human heights. I felt all this deeply, and, as I now
know, I behaved quite correctly during that moment. The Principal, who had come close to me, then said as follows: "There's
something important about you, Jakob." He stopped, and at once
I felt why. He doubtless wanted to see how I would now behave.
I noticed this and therefore I didn't move a muscle in my face, but
looked ahead, rigidly, mindlessly. Then we looked at one another
again. I stared austerely and sternly at my Principal. I managed
to sham coldness, superficiality, while in fact I'd have liked best

to laugh in his face for joy. But at the same time I saw that he was satisfied with my bearing, and finally he said: "My boy, go back to your work! Get busy with something. Or go and talk to Kraus. Go now!" I bowed deeply, just as usual, and went out. In the corridor I stopped, as once before, but actually also as usual, and listened at the keyhole, to hear if anything was going on in there. But everything was quiet. I couldn't help laughing softly and happily, a very silly laugh, and then I went into the class-room, where I saw Kraus sitting in the twilight, a brownish light seemed to surround him. I stood there for a long time. Really, I stood there a long time, for there was something, something that I couldn't quite understand. I felt as if I were at home. No, it was as if I hadn't yet been born, as if I were swimming in some element before birth. I felt hot and before my eyes there was a sea-like vagueness. I went to Kraus and said to him: "Kraus, I love you." He growled what's-all-this-about. Quickly I went up to my room. And now? Are we friends? Are Herr Benjamenta and I friends? In any case there's a relationship between us, but of what kind? I forbid myself to try to explain it. I want to keep bright, light, and happy. Away with thoughts!

I still haven't found a position. Herr Benjamenta says he's look-ing for one. He says so in a peremptory tone, and adds: "What? Impatient? All in good time. Wait!" The pupils are saying that Kraus will soon be departing. Departing, that sounds comically professional. Is Kraus going away soon? I hope these are only empty rumors, institutional excitements. Even among us pupils there's a kind of newspaper gossip, snatched out of air and empti-ness. The words, I notice, are everywhere the same. Also I have visited my brother again, and this fellow had the courage to introduce me to people. I sat at the tables of the rich, and I'll never forget the way I behaved. I was wearing an old, but still rather grand, frock coat. Frock coats make one old and important. So it was, and I acted like a man with an income of at least twenty thousand. I have talked with people who would have turned their backs on me if they could have guessed who I am. Women who would have despised me completely if I had told them that I'm only a pupil have smiled at me and have, as it were, made gestures of encouragement to me. And I was amazed at my appetite. How placidly one helps oneself at other people's tables! I saw how they all did it, and I copied them, with great talent. How vulgar that is. I feel something like shame to have shown my happy eating and drinking face there, in those particular circles. I didn't notice much in the way of refined manners. But I did notice that people thought of me as a timorous boy, whereas (in my own eyes) I was bursting with impudence. Johann behaves well in society. He has the light and pleasant manner of a man who is of some importance and who knows it. His behavior is a delight for the eyes that behold it. Do I speak too well of Johann? Oh, no. I'm not enamoured of my brother at all, but I try to see him whole, not only half. Of course, that may be love. No matter. It was very nice in the theater, too, but I don't want to enlarge on that. Then I took off the fine frock coat again. Oh, it's nice to walk and whizz around in the clothes of a person one esteems! Yes, whizz! One chirps and whizzes around there, in cultivated circles. Then I crept back to the Institute again and into my school clothes. I like it here and I shall probably have a foolish yearning for the Benjamentas later on, when I've become something grand, but I shall never, never be anything grand, and I tremble with a peculiar satisfaction that I should know this for certain in advance. One day I shall be laid low by a stroke, and then everything, all these confusions, this longing, this unknowing, all this, the gratitude and ingratitude, this telling lies and self-deception, this thinking that one knows and yet never knowing anything, will come to an end. But I want to live, no matter how.

Something incomprehensible has happened. Perhaps it's of no significance at all. I'm not much inclined to let myself be overcome by mysteries. I was sitting all alone in the schoolroom, it was almost nightfall. Suddenly Fräulein Benjamenta was standing behind me. I hadn't heard her come in, so she must have opened the door very quietly. She asked me what I was doing, but in a tone of voice that made an answer unnecessary. She said, as it were, even in asking, that she already knew. When that happens, one naturally doesn't answer. She placed a hand on my shoulder, as if she were tired and needed a support. Then I felt strongly that I belonged to her, that's to say, or is it, that I *did* belong to her? Yes, simply belonged to her. I always distrust feelings. But here my sort of belonging to her, to the Fräulein, was a true feeling. We belonged together. Naturally there was a difference. But suddenly we were close. Always, always, the difference. I really hate feeling little or no difference. To sense that Fräulein Benjamenta and I were two different kinds of being, in different situations, this was a joy for me. I usually despise deceiving myself. I consider distinctions and advantages as my enemies, unless they are completely genuine. So there was this big difference. Now what's all this? Can't I get over certain differences? But then the Fräulein said: "Come with me! Stand up and come with me. I want to show you something." We walked along together. Before our eyes, at least before mine (not hers, perhaps), everything was veiled in impenetrable darkness. "It's the inner chambers," I thought, and I wasn't wrong, either. That's how it was, and my dear instructress seemed to be resolved to show me a world that had been hidden until now. But I must pause for breath.

It was, as I said, completely dark at first. The Fräulein took me by the hand and said in a friendly voice: "Look, Jakob, there will be darkness all around you. And then someone will take you by the hand. And you will be glad of this and you will feel deep gratitude for the first time. Don't be disheartened. There will be brightnesses too." She had hardly said this when a white dazzling light shone toward us. A door appeared and we went, she in front and me close behind, through the opening, into the glorious fire of the light. Never had I seen anything so radiant and promising, so I was really quite stunned. The Fräulein spoke with a smile, in an even more friendly voice: "Does the light dazzle you? Then make every effort to endure it. It means joy and one must know how to feel and endure it. You can also think, if you like, that it means your future happiness, but look what's happening? It's disappearing. The light is falling to pieces. So, Jakob, you'll have no long-enduring happiness. Does my frankness hurt you? No. Come further now. We must hurry a little, for we must walk and tremble through several other apparitions. Tell me, Jakob, do you understand my words? But don't say anything. You're not allowed to talk here. Do you think that I'm an enchantress? No, I'm not an enchantress. To be sure, I know how to enchant a little, to seduce, I know that much. Every girl knows how to do that. But come on now." With these words the admirable girl opened a trap door in the floor, I had to help her, and we climbed together, she as ever in front, down into a deep cellar. At length, as the stone stairs came to an end, we were walking over moist, soft earth. I felt that we were standing in the middle of the earth's sphere, so deep and lonely was the place. We walked along a dark, lengthy corridor. Fräulein Benjamenta said: "We are now in the vaults of poverty and deprivation, and since you, dear Jakob, will probably be poor all your life, please try now to get a little accustomed to the darkness and to the cold, penetrating odor of the place. Don't be afraid, and don't be angry. God is here, too, he's everywhere. One must learn to love and nourish necessity. Kiss the wet earth of the cellar. I ask you, yes, do it. Thus you give the token of your willing submission to the heaviness and darkness which will, it seems, make up the greatest part of your life." I obeyed her, threw myself down on the cold earth and kissed it ardently, whereupon a hot and cold shudder ran through me. We walked on. Ah, these corridors of compulsory suffering and of terrible deprivation seemed endless to me, and perhaps they really were endless. The seconds were like whole lifetimes, and the minutes took on the size of anguished centuries. Enough, at last we reached a mournful wall, the Fräulein said: "Go and fondle the wall. It is the Wall of Worries. It will always stand before your eyes, and you'll be unwise to hate it. Ah, one must simply know how to avoid rigidity and whatever yields to no conciliation. Go and try it." I went quickly, as if in a passionate hurry, up to the wall and flung myself against its breast. Yes, against the stony breast, and I spoke to it a few kindly, almost joking words. And it remained unmoved, as was to be expected. I play-acted, to please my instructress, certainly, and yet again it was anything but play-acting that I was doing. And yet we both smiled, she, the instructress, as well as I, her callow pupil. "Come on," she said, "let's treat ourselves to a little freedom now, a little movement." And with her small white familiar cane she touched the wall, and the whole horrible cellar disappeared and we found ourselves on a smooth, spacious, narrow track of ice or glass. We floated along it, as if on marvelous skates, and we were dancing, too, for like a wave the track rose and fell beneath us. It was delightful. I had never seen anything like it and I shouted for joy: "How glorious!" And overhead the stars were shimmering, in a sky that was strangely all pale blue and yet dark, and the moon with its unearthly light was staring down upon us skaters. "This is freedom," said the instructress, "it's something very wintry, and cannot be borne for long. One must always keep moving, as we are doing here, one must dance in freedom. It is cold and beautiful. Never fall in love with it! That would only make you sad afterwards, for one can only be in the realm of freedom for a moment, no longer. Look how the wonderful track we are floating on is slowly melting away. Now you can watch freedom dying, if you open your eyes. You will have your full share of this agonizing sight later in life." Hardly had she spoken when we sank from our summit of happiness down into a place that was tired and cosy, it was a small bedchamber, chockfull of sophisticated comforts, tapestried with all kinds of wanton scenes and pictures. It was a proper pillowy boudoir. Often I had dreamed of real boudoirs. And now I was inside one of them. Music was rippling down around the walls like a graceful snowfall, one could even see the music being made, the notes like magical flakes of snow. "Here," said the Fräulein, "you can rest. You must decide for yourself how long." We both smiled at these mysterious words, and although an unspeakably slight fear stole up on me, I wasted no time in making myself comfortable in this chamber on one of the rugs that lay around. An uncommonly good-tasting cigarette flew down from above into my involuntarily opened mouth, and I smoked. A novel fluttered into my hands and I could read it undisturbed. "That's not the right thing for you. Don't read such books. Stand up. It's better we move on. Softness seduces one to thoughtlessness and cruelty. Listen, can't you hear their angry thunder, they're coming. This room is the chamber of calamity. You have had your repose in it. Now calamity will rain down on you and doubt and restlessness will drench you through. Come on! One must go out and meet the inevitable, bravely." Thus spoke the instructress and she had hardly finished when I was swimming in a gluey and most unpleasant river of doubt. Thoroughly disheartened, I didn't dare to look around to see if she was still near to me. No, the instructress, the enchantress who had conjured up all these visions and states, had disappeared. I was swimming all alone. I tried to scream, but the water only started to flow into my mouth. Oh, these calamities. I wept, and I bitterly regretted my surrender to the wanton pleasures of easefulness. Then suddenly I was sitting in the Benjamenta Institute again, in the dark classroom, and Fräulein Benjamenta was still standing behind me, and she stroked my cheeks, but as if she needed to comfort herself, not me. "She's unhappy," I thought. Then Kraus, Schacht, and Schilinski, who had been out together, came back. Quickly the girl drew her hand away from me and went into the kitchen to get supper. Had I been dreaming? But why ask myself this, now that it's time for supper? There are times when I simply love to eat. I can bite into the silliest foods then, just like a hungry young apprentice, then I am living in a fairy tale and am no longer a cultured being in an age of culture.

Sometimes our gymnastic and dancing classes are very amusing. To have to show skill is not without its dangers. What a fool one can make of oneself. To be sure, we pupils don't make fun of each other. We don't? Oh, yes, we do. One laughs with one's ears, if one isn't allowed to laugh with one's mouth. And with one's eyes. Eyes are very fond of laughing. And to make rules for the eyes, that's quite possible, to be sure, but pretty difficult. Thus, for example, we aren't allowed to wink, winking is mocking and therefore to be spurned, but one certainly does wink sometimes. To repress nature completely can't be done. And yet it can. But even if one has shed nature entirely, there's always a breath of it left, a remnant, and it shows. Beanpole Peter, for example, finds it very difficult to shed his own most personal nature. Sometimes when he's supposed to be dancing, moving gracefully and showing how graceful he is, he consists entirely of wood, and wood is Peter's natural state, like a gift of God. Yet one can't help laughing at a rafter when it appears in the form of a tall person, one has a glorious inside laugh. Laughter is the opposite of a piece of wood, it's something inflammatory, something that strikes matches inside you. Matches giggle, exactly like a repressed laugh. I very much like stopping the outburst of laughter. It tickles, marvelously: not letting it go, the thing that so much wants to come shooting out, I like things that aren't allowed to be, things that have to go down into my inside. It makes these repressed things more awkward, but at the same time more valuable. Yes, yes, I admit I like being repressed. To be sure. No, not always to be sure. On your way, Toby Shaw! What I mean is: if you aren't allowed to do something, you do it twice as much somewhere else. Nothing's more insipid than an indifferent, quick, cheap bit of permission. I like earning everything, experiencing everything, and a laugh, for example, also needs to be thoroughly experienced. When inside me I'm bursting with laughter, when I hardly know what to do with all this hissing gunpowder, then I know what laughing is, then I have laughed most laughishly, then I have a complete idea of what was shaking me. So I must firmly suppose and keep it as my strong conviction that rules do gild existence, or at least they silver it, in a word, they make it delectable. For certainly it's the same with almost all other things and pleasures as it is with the forbidden delectable laugh. Not being allowed to cry, for example, well, that makes crying larger. Doing without love, yes, that means loving. If I oughtn't to love, I love ten times as much. Everything that's forbidden lives a hundred times over; thus, if something is supposed to be dead, its life is all the livelier. As in small things, so in big ones. Nicely put, in everyday words, but in everyday things the true truths are found. I'm gabbling somewhat again, aren't I? I admit that I'm gabbling, but the lines have got to be filled with something. Forbidden fruits, how delectable, how delectable they are!

Perhaps now between Herr Benjamenta and me, visible to us both, a sort of forbidden fruit is hanging. But neither of us says anything openly, and that is certainly to be approved of. To me, for instance, friendly treatment is unpleasant. I mean generally. Certain people who feel affection for me are repulsive to me, I can't emphasize this overmuch. Naturally, I'm not averse to gentleness, and to warmth of heart. Who could be so crude as to shun completely all intimacy, all warmish feelings? But I'm always cautious about coming close to people, and I don't know, but I must have some sort of gift for convincing others, silently, that a closer approach would be unwise, at least I think it's difficult for anyone to steal into my confidence. And my warmth is precious to me, and anyone who wants to have it must be extremely cautious, and it's this that the Principal wants now. This Herr Benjamenta, it seems, wants to possess my heart and make friends with me. But for the present I'm treating him very coldly indeed, and who knows: perhaps I don't want to have anything to do with him.

"You're young," the Principal says to me, "you're bursting with prospects. Wait a moment, was there something else I forgot to say? You must realize, Jakob, that I've got a lot of things to say to you, and yet you can have forgotten the best and deepest things before you know where you are. And you yourself, you look like good fresh memory itself, whereas my memory is getting old now. My mind, Jakob, is dying. Forgive me if I'm saying things that are too weak, too intimate. It's a laugh. So I ask you to forgive me, whereas I could give you a good beating if I thought it necessary. What stern looks you're giving me. Well, well, I could throw you against that wall there, so hard you'd never see or hear anything again. I don't know what's happened to make me lose all my authority over you. Probably you laugh at me, secretly. But between ourselves: watch out. You must realize that wild feelings seize me sometimes and before I can stop myself I forget what I'm doing. O my little lad, no, don't be afraid. It would be so completely impossible, completely, to do you any harm, but—well, now, what was it I meant to say to you? Tell me, are you just a little frightened? And you're young and you've got hopes, and soon you want to find a position. Isn't that so? Yes, that's it. Yes, that's it and I'm sorry, for just think, sometimes I feel that you're my young brother or something near as nature to me, you seem so related to me, with your gestures, talk, mouth, everything, in short, yourself. I'm a king who's been deposed. You're smiling? I find it simply delightful, you know, that precisely when I'm talking about kings deposed and deprived of their thrones a smile escapes you, such a mischievous smile. You have intelligence, Jakob. Oh, it's so nice to be talking to you. It's a delightful prickly feeling to behave with you in a rather weak sort of way and more softly than usual. Yes, you really do provoke easy going, loosening up, the sacrifice of dignity. One attributes to you—do you believe me?—a nobility of mind, and this tempts one very strongly to indulge, when you are there, in fine and helpful explanations and confessions, as I do, for example, your master, confessing to you, my poor young worm, whom I could utterly crush if I chose to. Give me your hand. Good! Let me tell you that you've managed to make me feel respect for you. I respect you highly, and—I—don't mind—telling you. And now I want to ask you something: will you be my friend, the small sharer of my confidences? I ask you, please do. But I'll give you time to think it over, you may go now. Please go, leave me alone." That's the way my Principal speaks to me, the man who, as he says himself, could utterly crush me just when he chooses. I don't bow to him any more, it would hurt his feelings. What was that he was saying about deposed kings? I'll waste no time thinking about all this, as he recommends, but I shall simply carry on maintaining the formalities. In any case, it means I must watch out. He talks about wildness? Well, I must say, that's very disturbing. I'm much too good to be squashed against a wall. Shall I tell the Fräulein? Good heavens, no. I've got enough courage to keep silent about something that's strange, and enough intelligence to cope with something dubious alone. Perhaps Herr Benjamenta is mad. In any case, he's like the lion, but I'm the mouse. A nice state of affairs in the Institute now. Only I mustn't tell anyone. Sometimes a thing that's kept hidden is an advantage gained. It's all quite silly. Basta!

What strange imaginings I sometimes have! They're almost quite absurd. Suddenly, without my being able to stop it, I had become a commander in the war around the year 1400, no, a bit later, at the time of the Milan campaigns. I and my officers, we were having dinner. It was after a victory in battle, and our fame would be spreading throughout Europe during the next few days. We were drinking and making merry. We were dining not in a room, no, but out of doors. The sun was just setting, then before my eyes, whose ray meant the start of battle and victory in arms, a creature was brought, a poor devil, a captured traitor. The unhappy man bowed his head and was trembling, knowing that he had no right to look at the commander-in-chief. I looked at him, quite fleetingly, then I looked just as lightly and fleetingly at the men who had brought him along, then I devoted myself to the full glass of wine before me, and these three movements meant: "Take him away and hang him!" At once the people seized him, and then the poor fellow screamed in desperation, worse, as if he was being torn apart, torn apart already by a thousand dreadful martyrs' deaths. My ears had heard all kinds of sounds in the fights and battles that filled my life, and my eyes were more than accustomed to the sight of terrible and painful things, but strangely enough, this was something I couldn't endure. Once more I turned to the condemned man, also I gestured to the soldiers. "Let him go," I said, the glass at my lips, to make it short. Then something at once moving and repulsive happened. The man to whom I had given back his life, his criminal's and traitor's life, plunged madly to my feet and kissed the dust on my shoes. I thrust him away. I was overcome with disgust and horror. I was stirred by the power at my command, the power with which I could freely play, as the gale plays with leaves, stirred so that it hurt, so I laughed and ordered the man to go away. He was almost out of his mind. A bestial joy gushed from eyes and mouth, he babbled thanks, thanks, and crawled away. Until late in the night we others gave ourselves up to wild drinking and revelry, and early in the morning, as we still sat at the table, I received with a dignity, a grandeur that nearly made even me smile, the emissaries of the Pope. I was the hero, the master of the day. On my whim, my satisfaction, depended the peace of half of Europe. Yet for the diplomatic gentlemen I played the fool, the kind fool, it suited me that way, I was a bit tired, I wanted to go home. I allowed the advantages won in war to be taken away from me. Naturally I was later made a Count, then I got married, and now I have sunk so low that I'm not troubled at all to be a humble little pupil at the Benjamenta Institute, and to have friends like Kraus, Schacht, and Schilinski. Throw me naked on the cold street and perhaps I'll imagine that I'm the all-embracing Lord God. It's time I laid down my pen.

For such small and humble people as us pupils there is nothing comic. Without dignity, one takes everything in a serious way, but also lightly, almost frivolously. For me our classes in dancing, propriety, gymnastics, seem like public life itself, large, important, and then before my eyes the schoolroom is transformed into a splendid drawing room, into a street full of people, into a castle with old long corridors, into an official chamber, into a scholar's study, into a lady's reception room, it just depends, it can be anything. We must enter, make formal greeting, bow, speak, deal with imaginary business matters or tasks, carry out orders, then suddenly we're at table and dining in a metropolitan manner and servants are waiting on us. Schacht, or perhaps even Kraus, pretends to be a lady of the high aristocracy, and I undertake to entertain her. Then we are all cavaliers, not excluding Beanpole Peter, who always feels that he's a cavalier anyway. Then we dance. We hop around, followed by the laughing gaze of the instructress, and suddenly we rush to the aid of a casualty. He has been run over on the street. We give some small charity to a beggar, write letters, bellow at our valets, go to meetings, visit places where French is spoken, practice doffing our hats, talk about hunting, finance, and art, submissively kiss the five outstretched pretty fingers of ladies whom we want to feel fond of us, loaf like lay-abouts, quaff coffee, eat hams cooked in Burgundy, sleep in imaginary beds, get up again apparently early in the morning, say, "Good day, Judge," fight with one another, for that happens in life too, and simply do all the things that occur in life. If we get tired of all of these follies, the Fräulein taps her cane on the edge of her desk and says: "*Allons,* come on, boys! Work!" Then we work at it again. We cruise around the room like wasps. It's quite hard to describe, and if we get tired again, the instructress calls: "What? Are you sick of public life already? Get on with it! Show how life is. It's easy, but you must be brisk, or life will tread on you." And briskly off we go again. We travel, and our servants do silly things. We sit in libraries and study. We are soldiers, genuine recruits, and we must lie down and shoot. We walk into shops, to buy things, into swimming places, to swim, into churches, to pray: "Lord, lead us not into temptation." And the next moment we are slap in the middle of the crassest error, and committing sins. "Stop. Enough for today," the instructress then says, when it's time. Then life is extinguished and the dream called human life takes another course. Usually then I go for half an hour's walk. A girl always meets me in the park, where I sit on a bench. She seems to be a shopgirl. She always cranes her neck around and gives me a long look. She's always swooning. It happens that she thinks I'm a gentleman earning a monthly salary. I look so good, like the right sort of thing. She's wrong, and that's why I ignore her.

Now and again we also act plays, comedies, to be precise, which deteriorate into farce, until the instructress signals us to stop. The Mother: "I cannot give you my daughter for a wife, you are too poor." The Hero: "Poverty is no disgrace." The Mother: "Fiddlesticks! That's empty talk. What are your prospects?" The Loving Girl: "Mamma, I must ask you, with all due respect, to speak more politely to the man whom I love." The Mother: "Silence! One day you'll be grateful to me for treating him with ruthless severity. Now, sir, tell me, where did you do your studies?" The Hero (he is Polish, and is played by Schilinski): "I graduated at the Benjamenta Institute, gracious lady. Forgive me for the pride with which I speak these words." The Daughter: "Ah, Mamma, just see how well he behaves. What refined manners." The Mother (severely): "Don't talk to me about manners. Aristocratic behavior doesn't matter a fig nowadays. You, sir, please would you tell me this: What did you learn at the Bagnamenta Institute?" The Hero: "Forgive me, but the Institute is called Benjamenta, not Bagnamenta. What did I learn? Well, of course, I must confess that I learned very little there. But learning a lot doesn't matter a fig nowadays. You yourself must admit that." The Daughter: "You heard what he said, Mamma dear?" The Mother: "Don't talk to me, you little wretch, about hearing such nonsense or even taking it seriously. Now, my pretty young gentleman, you would do me a favor if you removed yourself from my sight, once and for all." The Hero: "What's this you venture to offer me? Oh, well, so be it. Adieu, I'm going." Exit, et cetera. The content of our little dramas always relates to the school and the pupils. A pupil experiences all kinds of mixed and various fates, bad and good. He has success in the world, or total failure. A play always ends with a glorification and tableau of humble service. Happiness serves: that is the lesson of our dramatic literature. Our Fräulein usually represents, during the performance, the world of the spectators. She sits, as it were, in her box and gazes through her eyeglasses down upon the stage, that's to say, upon us actors. Kraus is the worst actor. Acting doesn't suit him at all. The best is definitely Beanpole Peter. Heinrich, too, is charming on the stage.

I have the somewhat unpleasant feeling that I shall always have something to eat in the world. I'm healthy, and shall remain so, and people will always be able to make use of me somehow. I shall never be a burden to my nation, or my community. To think this, that's to say, to think that as a humble person one will always have one's daily bread to eat, would deeply wound me if I were the earlier Jakob von Gunten, if I were still the descendant, scion of the house, but I have become a quite quite different person, I have become an ordinary person, and I have to thank the Benjamentas for my becoming ordinary, and this fills me with a confidence beyond words, that shines with the

dew of contentment. I've changed my pride, my kinds of honor.
How have I come to be degenerate so young? But is this degener-
ation? To some extent it is, in other ways it's the preservation of
my kind of being. Perhaps I shall remain, lost and forgotten somewhere else in life, a purer and prouder von Gunten than if I were
to have stayed at home, pecking at the family tree, rotting, heart-
less, ossified. Well, be that as it may. I have made the choice and
there it is. There's a strange energy in me, an urge to learn life
from the roots, and an irrepressible desire to provoke people and
things into revealing themselves to me. This makes me think of
Herr Benjamenta. But I want to think of something else, that's to
say, I don't want to think of anything.

        I have met quite a number of people, thanks to
Johann's friendliness. There are artists among them, and they
seem to be pleasant people. Well, what can one say after such
fleeting contact? Actually, people who make efforts to be successful are terribly like each other. They all have the same face. Not
really, and yet they do. They're all alike in their rapid kindness,
which just comes and goes, and I think this is because of the fear
which these people feel. They deal with persons and objects, one
after the other, only so that they can cope again with some new
thing that also seems to be demanding attention. They don't
despise anyone, these good people, and yet perhaps they despise
everything, but they aren't allowed to show it, because they're
frightened of being suddenly incautious. They're kind out of
Weltschmerz and pleasant out of fear. And then everyone wants
to be respected. These people are cavaliers. And they seem never
to feel quite right. Whoever can feel right if he places value on the
tokens of respect and the distinctions conferred by the world? And

then I think that these people, who are, after all, society people and not living in a state of nature, are always feeling that some successor is pursuing them. Everyone senses the awful ambush, the secret thief, who comes creeping up with some new gift or other, spreading damage and humiliations of every kind all around, and therefore in these circles the completely new person is the most sought-after and most preferred, and woe to the older ones if this new one is somehow distinguished by intelligence, talent, or natural genius. I'm expressing myself rather too simply. There's something quite different about it all. In these circles of progressive culture there's a fairly obvious and unmistakable fatigue. Not the formal blasé-ness, say, of an aristocracy of birth, no, but a genuine, a completely authentic fatigue that dwells in higher and more lively feelings, the fatigue of the healthy-unhealthy person. They're all cultivated, but do they respect one another? They are, if they think about it honestly, content with their positions in life, but are they really contented people? Of course, there are rich people among them. I'm not talking about them here, for the money a man has forces one to assume wholly different things when judging him. Yet they're all well-mannered people and, in their own way, important ones, and I must be extremely grateful to my brother for acquainting me with this bit of the world. Already in those circles people like to call me the little von Gunten, in contrast to Johann, whom they have christened the big von Gunten. These are jokes, the world just likes jokes. I don't, but it doesn't matter, all this. I feel how little it concerns me, everything that's called "the world," and how grand and exciting what I privately call the world is to me. My brother has tried to introduce me to people, and it's my duty to make much of this. And it is much, too. Even the smallest of things is much to me. To know a few people perfectly takes a lifetime. That's another of the Benjamenta precepts, and how unlike the world the Benjamentas are. I'm going to bed now.

I never forget that I'm a descendant beginning from all the way down, without having the qualities which one needs if one is going to rise to the top. Perhaps I have. Everything is possible, but I put no trust in the idle moments when I imagine happiness for myself, combined with splendor. I have none of the virtues of an upstart. I'm cheeky sometimes, but only as a passing mood. The upstart's cheekiness is a permanent shamming of modesty, or his gesture is that of cheeky, permanently cheeky insignificance. And there are many upstarts, and stupidly they cling to what they have attained, and that is excellent. They may also be nervous, indignant, peevish, and fed up with "all those things," but the fed-upness of the genuine upstart is nothing deep. Upstarts are masters, and perhaps as a descendant of my family, or whatever I am, I shall serve a master, perhaps a somewhat pompous master, and serve him honorably, loyally, reliably, steadfastly, without thinking, without the least concern for personal advantage, for only in this way, that is, with every decency, shall I be able to serve anyone at all, and now I notice that I've got something in common with Kraus, and I'm almost a little ashamed. Feelings like those with which I confront the world will never lead to great things, unless one snaps one's fingers at the sparkling grandeurs and calls that great which is quite grey, quiet, hard and humble. Yes, I shall serve and I shall always accept duties whose fulfillment is anything but a glitter, this will happen over and over again, and I shall blush with utter stupid joy if anyone says a flippant word of thanks. That is stupid but completely true, and I'm incapable of being sad about it. I must confess: I'm never sad, and I never feel lonely, never, and that is also stupid, for with sentimentality, with the thing that people call the cry from the heart, the best and most upstartish and topping business is done. But thanks very much for the trouble, for the indelicate effort it takes to reach an honorable status in such a way. At home, with father and mother, the whole house smelled of tact. Well, I don't mean literally. Things were genteel with us at home. And so bright. The entire household was like a gracious, kindly smile. Mamma is so refined. All right, then. I'm from that family and am condemned to be a servant and play a sixth-rate role in the world. In my view this is apt, for—oh, what did Johann say?— "The people with the power, they are the really starving people." I don't like to think that this is so. And do I need to console myself at all? Can anyone console a Jakob von Gunten? As long as I have a healthy body, there can be no question of it.

If I want to, if I tell myself to, I can revere everything, even bad behavior, but it must have the color of money. The bad manners would have to drop twenty-mark gold pieces behind them, then I'd bow to them, and behind them as well. Herr Benjamenta is of the same opinion. He says it's wrong to despise money and the advantages that fall from unlovely hands. A pupil at the Benjamenta Institute is supposed to respect most things, not to despise them.—Let's change the subject. Gymnastics, I like that. I love it passionately, and of course I'm good at it. To make friends with a noble person and to do gymnastics, these are probably the best things in the world. To dance and to find a person who engages my respect is one and the same thing for me. I like so much to set minds and limbs in motion. Just to kick

up one's legs, how nice that is! Gymnastics is silly, too, and leads
to nothing. Does everything I love and prefer have to lead to
nothing? But listen! What's that? Someone's calling for me. I
must stop.

"Are you still making honest endeavors, Jakob?"
the instructress asked me. It was toward evening. Somewhere
there was a reddish light, like the glow of an immense and lovely
sunset. We were standing by the door to my room. I'd gone there
a moment before, to ponder my dreams and forebodings a little.
"Fräulein Benjamenta," I said, "do you doubt the seriousness and
honesty of my endeavors? Am I, in your eyes, a swindler and a
cheat?" I think I was looking positively tragic as I said this. She
turned her beautiful face to me and said: "Heaven forbid. You're
a nice boy. You're impetuous, but you're decent and pleasant, I
like you, just as you are. Are you content? Are you? Well? Do you
make your bed properly every morning? Yes? And you stopped
obeying the rules long ago? You didn't? Or did you? Oh, you're a
very good boy, I believe you. And no praise could be fulsome
enough for you. Never. Whole buckets full of flattering praise,
just think, whole pitchers and pannikins full. One would have to
use a broom to sweep them all up. The many fine words of recognition for your behavior. No. Jakob, quite seriously now, listen.
I must whisper something to you. Do you want to hear it or would
you rather slip away into your room here?" "Tell me what it is,
Fräulein, I'm listening," I said, full of anxious expectation. Suddenly the instructress gave a great shudder. But quickly she controlled herself and said: "I must go, Jakob, I must go. And it
will go with me. I just can't tell it to you. Perhaps another time.
Yes? Yes, perhaps tomorrow, or in a week. It still won't be too

late to tell you then. Tell me, Jakob, do you love me a little? Do I mean anything to you, to your young heart?" She stood there in front of me, her lips pressed angrily together. I quickly stooped to her hand, which hung unspeakably sadly down against her dress, and kissed it. I was so happy to be allowed to tell her now what I had always felt for her. "Do you think highly of me?" she asked, the pitch of her voice rising till it was almost stifled and died away. I said: "How could you be in any doubt? I am unhappy." But I felt so outraged that I could have wept. I abruptly let go of her hand and stood there respectfully. And she went away, with an almost imploring look. How everything has changed in this once so tyrannical Benjamenta Institute! Everything's collapsing, the classes, the effort, the rules. Is this a morgue, or is it a celestial house of joy? Something is going on and I don't understand it yet.

I ventured to make a remark to Kraus about the Benjamentas. I said that I thought the old splendor of the Institute was clouding over. I asked what it meant, and if Kraus knew anything about it. He got angry and said: "You, you've got yourself pregnant with silly ideas. What a notion. Do something! Work, then you won't notice anything. You snooper. Snooping around for opinions and thoughts. Go away. I'm beginning to hate the sight of you." "You're getting a bit rude, aren't you?" I said, but I thought it better to leave him alone. During the day I had a chance to talk to Fräulein Benjamenta about Kraus. She said to me: "Yes, Kraus isn't like other people. He sits there till one needs him, if one calls him he gets moving and rushes up. One doesn't make much fuss about people like him. Actually, one never praises Kraus, and one is hardly grateful to him. One only asks of him, Do this or

Do that. And one hardly notices that he's been of service, and how excellently so, his service is that perfect. As a person, Kraus is nothing, Kraus is something as a doer, as a person for a job, but he doesn't make himself noticeable at all. You, for instance, Jakob, one praises you, it's a joy to make you feel good. One hasn't a word for Kraus, one feels no fondness for him. You're very nasty to Kraus, Jakob. You're nicer than he is, though. I won't put it any other way, for you wouldn't understand. And Kraus will be leaving us soon. That will be a loss, Jakob. Oh, that's a loss. If Kraus isn't there any more, who is there left? You, yes. That's true, and now you're angry with me, aren't you? Yes, you're angry with me, because I'm sad about Kraus leaving. Are you jealous?" "Not at all. I'm very sorry, too, about Kraus leaving us," I said. I spoke intentionally in a formal sort of way. I had begun to feel sad, too, but I found it proper to be a little cold. Later I tried to have a talk with Kraus, but he was still incredibly stand-offish. He sat glumly at the table and said nothing to anybody. He is also feeling that something's not quite right here, only he doesn't say anything, except to himself.

Often the feeling of a great inner defeat comes over me. When it does so, I position myself in the middle of the classroom and do silly things, quite childish silly things. I put Kraus's cap on my head, or a glass of water, et cetera. Or Hans is there. With Hans one can throw hats, trying to make them land on the other person's head and stick there. How Kraus despises us for this. Schacht has had a job for three days, but he has come back, very depressed and with all kinds of angry, painful excuses. Didn't I say earlier that things would go badly for Schacht out in the world? He will always wriggle into functions, tasks, and jobs and he won't like it anywhere. Now he says he had to work too hard, and he talks about cunning, malicious, and lazy halfway superiors who began to heap unfair duties on him mischievously the moment he arrived, and to torment him utterly and to cheat him. Ah, I believe Schacht. Only too willingly; that's to say, I think what he says is absolutely true, for the world is incomprehensibly crass, tyrannical, moody, and cruel to sickly and sensitive people. Well, Schacht will stay here for the time being. We laughed at him at bit, when he arrived, that can't be helped either, Schacht is young and after all he can't be allowed to think that there are special degrees, advantages, methods, and considerations for him. He has now had his first disappointment, and I'm convinced that he'll have twenty disappointments, one after the other. Life with its savage laws is in any case for certain people a succession of discouragements and terrifying bad impressions. People like Schacht are born to feel and suffer a continuous sense of aversion. He would like to admit and welcome things, but he just can't. Hardness and lack of compassion strike him with tenfold force, he just feels them more acutely. Poor Schacht. He's a child and he should be able to revel in melodies and bed himself in kind, soft, carefree things. For him there should be secret splashings and bird-song. Pale and delicate evening clouds should waft him away into the kingdom of Ah, What's Happening to Me? His hands are made for light gestures, not for work. Before him breezes should blow, and behind him sweet, friendly voices should be whispering. His eyes should be allowed to remain blissfully closed, and Schacht should be allowed to go quietly to sleep again, after being wakened in the morning in the warm, sensuous cushions. For him there is, at root, no proper activity, for every activity is for him, the way he is, improper, unnatural, and unsuitable. Compared with Schacht

I'm the trueblue rawboned laborer. Ah, he'll be crushed, and one day he'll die in a hospital, or he'll perish, ruined in body and soul, inside one of our modern prisons. Now he crouches around in the corners of the classroom, is ashamed of himself and trembling with dread of the repulsive unknown future. The Fräulein looks at him anxiously, but she's at present much too concerned with her very own peculiar affairs to be much troubled about Schacht. Anyway, she couldn't help him. A God would have to do that, and could do it perhaps, only there are no gods, only one, and he's too sublime to help. To help and to alleviate, that wouldn't be proper for the Almighty, at least that's how I feel.

Fräulein Benjamenta now says a few words to me every day, either in the kitchen or in the sometimes very quiet and empty classroom. Kraus is acting as if he reckoned on spending another decade here in the Institute. Dryly and fretfully he learns his lessons, yes, he really is fretful about it, but he always did look that way, it doesn't mean anything special. This person isn't capable of any overhastiness, or any impatience. "Wait for It" is written almost majestically on his tranquil brow. Yes, the Fräulein said this once, she said that Kraus has majesty, and it's true, the unassumingness of his character has something of an invisible emperor about it. To my Fräulein I ventured to say yesterday: "If my attitude to you has ever been a single time, for a tiny, shrinking, single moment, more self-possessed than swayed by feelings and bonds of the purest respect, I will hate myself, persecute myself, hang myself with a rope, poison myself with the deadliest poisons, cut my throat with knives, no matter of what sort. No, it's quite impossible, Fräulein. I could never do you any injury! Your very eyes. How they have always been for me the command to obey, the inviolable and beautiful commandment. No, no, I'm not telling lies. Your appearance in the doorway! I have never needed a heaven here, never needed moon, sun, and stars. You, yes, you, have been for me the higher presence. I'm speaking the truth, Fräulein, and I must assume that you can feel how far these words are from any kind of flattery. I hate all future success, I find life repugnant. Yes, yes. and yet soon I too must leave, like Kraus, and go out into hateful life. You have been my body's health. Whenever I have read a book, it was you I was reading, not the book, you were the book. You were, you were. Often I've behaved badly. Several times you had to warn me against the pride that was eating me up and trying to bury me under the ruins of improper imaginings. How it subsided then, as quick as lightning. How attentively I listened to what Fräulein Benjamenta was saying. You smile? Yes, your smile has always been a spur to goodness, courage, and truth. You have always been too kind to me! Much, much too kind for such a pig-head. And at the sight of you my many failings fell at your feet, imploring forgiveness. No, I don't want to go out into life, into the world. I despise everything that the future may hold in store. When you walked into the classroom, I was happy, and then I always scolded myself for being such a fool. Often— just think, yes, I must confess it—often, secretly, I thought to rob you of your dignity and grandeur, but I found in my raging spirit not a word, not a single little word with which to revile and reduce what it was I wanted to injure a little. And my punishment, every time, was my remorse and my restlessness. Yes, always, always I have had to revere you, Fräulein. Are you angry that I should speak to you so? I, I am happy to be speaking so." She looked at me with twinkling eyes and smiled. She was a bit scornful, but she was quite content. Moreover, she was preoccupied, I noticed, with some faraway thoughts. In spirit she was somewhere else, and therefore, only for that reason, did I dare to speak to her in this way. I shall take care not to do so again.

It's not my concern, I know, but it's a noticeable fact that no new pupils are entering the Institute. Is the reputation which Herr Benjamenta enjoyed in the world as an educator on the wane or even near to vanishing? That would be sad. But perhaps it's only because I'm over-sensitive. I've become a little nervous here, if that's what one can call it when one's powers of observation are at once excited and tired. Everything has become so fragile here, and it's as if one were standing in midair, not on firm ground. And then this being permanently prepared and alert, that does something too. It's quite possible. One's always waiting for something, well, that tends to weaken one. And, again, one forbids oneself to listen and wait for things, because it's not permissible. Well, that makes claims on one's powers as well. Often the Fräulein stands at the window and looks out for a long time, as if she were living somewhere else already. Yes, that's it, that's the somewhat unhealthy and unnatural way in which things are moving here: we're all, superiors and pupils, all nearly living somewhere else. It's as if we had only a little time left to breathe, sleep, wake up, and give and enjoy instruction here. There's something like a rushing, ruthless energy beating its wings and fluttering about the place. Are we all listening for what's to come? For some future happening? Also possible. And what if we present pupils all leave and no new ones arrive? What then? Will the Benjamentas be poor and forsaken? When I imagine this, I feel ill, simply ill. No, never, never! It shall never be allowed to happen. Yet it has to be. Has to be?

To be robust means not spending time on thought but quickly and quietly entering into what has to be done. To be wet with the rains of exertion, hard and strong from the knocks and rubs of what necessity demands. I hate such clever turns of phrase. I was intending to think of something quite different. Aha, yes, that's what it was, it's about Herr Benjamenta. I've been with him in the office again. I keep teasing him about the job I am to get, and soon. So this time I asked again how things stood now, if I could reckon . . . et cetera. He started to get furious. Oh, he keeps getting furious now, and I'm always very daring when I excite him. I asked in a very loud voice, abruptly and shamelessly. The Principal got very embarrassed, he even began to rub behind his big ears. Of course he hasn't got what people call big ears, his ears are relatively not big at all, it's just that everything about the man is big, consequently his ears are big too. At length he came up to me, gave a very kind-hearted laugh, and said: "You want to go out to work, Jakob? But I tell you, you'll do better to stay here. It's very nice here for you and people like you. Or isn't it? Stay on a little longer. I would even like to advise you to be a little torpid, forgetful, lazy-minded. For you see, what people call the vices play such a large role in human life, they're important, I might even say they're necessary. If there were no vices and failings, there'd be a shortage of warmth, charm, and richness in the world. Half of the world, and perhaps it is at root the better half, would perish along with the indolence and the weaknesses. No, be lazy. Well, well, now, don't misunderstand me, be just as you are, just as you have come to be, but please play at being a little remiss. Will you do it? Yes? It would please me to see you given to dreaming a little. Hang your head, be pensive, look

gloomy, won't you? Because for my taste you're a little bit too full
of will power, too full of character. And you're proud, Jakob!
What's your attitude, really? Do you think you'll attain and
achieve great things out there in the world? That you have to do
so? Do you seriously intend to do something important? You almost give me this unfortunately somewhat vehement impression.
Or do you perhaps, perhaps out of defiance, want to remain very
small? I can believe that of you as well. You're in rather a too festive, too violent, too triumphal state. But none of that matters,
you'll stay for a while, Jakob. I'm not going to find a job for you,
I won't do any such thing for you, not for a long time. Do you
know, what I want is to keep you. I've hardly got you for myself
and you want to run away? That can't be done. Get bored here in
the Institute as well as you can. Oh, you little world-conqueror,
out in the world, out there, in a profession, endeavoring, achiev-
ing things, whole seas of boredom, emptiness, loneliness will yawn
at you. Stay here. Go on yearning for a bit longer. You've no idea
what bliss, what grandeur there is in yearning, in waiting. So wait.
Let it press on you inside, all the same. But not too much. Listen,
if you left it would hurt me, it would wound me, quite incurably,
it would almost kill me. Kill me? Now you have a good laugh at
me, go on. Laugh me utterly to scorn, Jakob. You have my permission. Yet, tell me, what is there that I can order or permit you to
do in future? I, who have just convinced you that I'm almost, almost dependent on you? I've started something that makes me
shudder, that outrages me and at the same time makes me happy,
Jakob. But, for the first time, I love somebody. But you don't understand that. Go away now! Be off with you. You insolent fellow, remember that I can still punish. Watch out!" Well, there
it was, suddenly he had got furious again. I quickly disappeared

from under his dark, penetrating gaze. What eyes he has! The Principal's eyes. I must here observe that I have incredible skill in flitting out of places. I positively flew out of the office, no, I whistled out of it, as the wind whistles, when the gentleman said to me: "Watch out!" Oh, yes, one sometimes can't help feeling frightened of him. I'd find it improper if I weren't frightened, for then I'd have no courage, since courage is precisely the thing that comes of conquering fear. Once more, out in the corridor, I listened at the keyhole, and again it was all quiet in there. I even stuck out my tongue, in a quite childish and schoolboyish way, and then I couldn't help laughing. I think I've never laughed so much in all my life. Very quietly, of course. It was the purest repressed laugh imaginable. When I laugh like that, well, then there's nothing more that's above me. Then I'm the unbeatable embracer and ruler of all things. At such moments I'm simply grand.

Yes, that is how it is: I'm still at the Benjamenta Institute, I must still go in fear of the existing statutes, lessons are still being given, questions are asked and answered, we still fly to commands, Kraus still knocks in the mornings on my door, with his peevish "Get up, Jakob" and his angrily raised forefinger, we pupils still say "Good day, Fräulein" when she appears and "Good night" when she retires in the evening. We're still caught in the iron talons of the numerous rules and indulge in didactic, monotonous repetitions. Also I've been, at last, in the authentic inner chambers, and I must say, they don't exist. There are two rooms, but these two rooms don't look chamber-like at all. The furniture is frugal and ordinary in the extreme, and there's nothing mysterious about them at all. Strange. How did I get the mad idea that the Benjamentas live in chambers? Or was I dreaming, and is the dream over now? As a matter of fact, there are goldfish there and Kraus and I regularly have to empty and clean the tank in which these animals swim and live, and then fill it with fresh water. But is there anything remotely magical about that? Goldfish can occur in any middling Prussian official's family, and there's nothing incomprehensible and unusual about the families of officials. Wonderful! And I believed in the inner chambers so steadfastly. I thought that beyond the door through which the Fräulein passes to and fro there would be hundreds of castle rooms and apartments. In my mind I saw delicately coiling spiral stairways and other broad stone staircases laid with carpets, behind that simple door. Also an ancient library was there, and corridors, long and serene corridors with floor mats, ran in my imagination from one end of the building to the other. With all my ideas and follies I could one day found a corporate company for the propagation of beautiful but unreliable imaginings. The capital's there, it seems to me, there will be funds enough, and buyers of such shares are to be found wherever the idea of beauty and belief in it have not quite perished. What things I imagined! A park, of course. I can't live without a park. Also a chapel, only, strangly enough, not a romantically ruined one, but a smartly restored one, a small Protestant house of God. The parson was having breakfast. And all that sort of thing. People dined, and arranged hunts. Evenings they danced in the baronial hall, on whose high walls of dark wood hung the portraits of family ancestors. What family? I stammer that word, for in fact I can't say it. No, I deeply regret having dreamed up these fantasies. I saw snow flying too, into the castle courtyard. There were large wet snowflakes, and it was early in the morning, the time was always early on a dark winter morning. Ah, and there was something else beautiful, a hall, yes, I saw a hall. Fascinating! Three noble old dames were sitting beside a tittering and crackling fire. They were doing crochet work. What kind of a fantasy is that, not to be able to see further than where people are knitting and crocheting! But it was just this that enraptured me. If I had enemies, they'd say that it was morbid, and they'd think they had reason to shun me along with the dear cosy crochet work as well. Then there was a wonderful nocturnal feast, with candles shining down from silver candelabra. The joyous table sparkled and dazzled and talked. I thought that was really beautiful. And women, what women. One looked like a veritable princess, and she was one, too. There was an Englishman there. How the feminine garments rustled, how the breasts, naked, rose and fell! The diningroom was crisscrossed with perfumes in snakelike lines. The splendor was allied with modesty, the tact with pleasure, the joy with refinement, and the elegance was festooned with nobility of birth. Then it all swam away, the other things came, new things. Yes, the inner chambers, they were alive, and now it's as if they've been stolen away from me. Bare reality: what a crook it sometimes is. It steals things, and afterwards it has no idea what to do with them. It just seems to spread sorrow for fun. Of course, I like sorrow very much as well, it's very valuable, very. It shapes one.

Heinrich and Schilinski have left. Shaken hands and said adieu. And gone. Probably forever. How short these leave-takings are! One means to say something, but has forgotten precisely the right thing to say, and so one says nothing, or something silly. To say goodbye, and to have it said to me, is terrible. At such moments something gives human life a shake, and one feels vividly how nothing one is. Quick goodbyes are loveless, and long ones are unbearable. What can one do? Well, one just says something goofish.—Fräulein Benjamenta said something very peculiar to me. "Jakob," she said, "I am dying. Don't be afraid. Let me talk to you quite calmly. Tell me, why have you become my confidant like this? From the start, when you arrived here, I thought you were nice, and sensitive. Please don't make any falsely honest objections. You're vain. Are you vain? Listen, soon it will be over with me. Can you keep a secret? You must say nothing about what I'm going to tell you. Above all, your Principal, my brother, mustn't know anything, make a point of remembering that. But I'm quite calm, and so are you, and you'll keep your word and keep your mouth shut, I know. Something is gnawing at me, and I'm sinking down into something, and I know what that means. It's so sad, my dear young friend, so sad. I think you're strong, don't I, Jakob? But I know it, I know you're strong. You have a heart. Kraus wouldn't listen to everything I had to say. I find it so nice that you aren't crying. Oh, I'd find it repulsive if just now your eyes were to moisten over. That can wait. And you listen so nicely. You listen to my miserable tale as if it were something small, fine, and ordinary, something that attracts attention only, but no more, that's how you're listening. You can behave immensely well, if you take the trouble. Of course, you're arrogant, we know that, don't we? Quiet, now, not a murmur. Yes, Jakob, death (oh, what a word) is standing behind me. Look, like this, the way I breathe on you, that's how he's breathing his cold, horrible breath at me from behind, and I'm sinking, sinking because of this breath. My breast is pressing it out of me. Have I made you feel sad? Tell me. Is this sad for you? A little, isn't it? But now you must forget it all, do you hear? Forget it! I'll come to you again, like today, and then I'll tell you how I am. You'll try to forget it, won't you? But come here. Let me touch your forehead. You're a good boy."—She drew me gently toward her and pressed something like a breath on my forehead. It was nothing like the touch that she spoke of. Then she quietly went away and I surrendered to my thoughts. Thoughts? Not really. I thought once more of my not having any money. That was my thought. That's how I am, so crude, and so thoughtless. And it's like this: heartfelt emotions put something like any icy coldness into my soul. If there's immediate cause for sadness, the feeling of sadness entirely escapes me. I don't like to tell lies. And to tell them to myself: what point would that have? I tell lies somewhere else, but not here, not in front of myself. No, it beats me, but here I am, alive, and Fräulein Benjamenta says such a terrifying thing, and I, who worship her, I can't shed a single tear? I'm mean, that's what it is. But stop. I don't intend to disparage myself too much. I'm puzzled, and therefore—. It's lies, all lies. Actually I knew it all along. Knew it? That's another lie. It's not possible for me to tell myself the truth. Anyway, I shall obey the Fräulein and say nothing about this. To be allowed to obey her! As long as I obey her, she will live.

Assuming I were a soldier (and by nature I'm an excellent soldier), an ordinary infantryman, and serving under the banners of Napoleon, then one day I would march off to Russia. I would get on well with my comrades, because the misery, the deprivations, and our many rough deeds would forge us into something like a mass of iron. Grimly we would stare ahead. Yes, grimness, dull, unconscious anger, would unite us. And we would march, always with our rifles slung on our shoulders. In the cities through which we passed, an idle, drooping crowd of people would gape at us, demoralized by the tramp of our feet. And then there would be no more cities, or just very seldom, only unending stretches of country would crawl away to the horizon before our eyes and legs. The country would positively crawl and creep. And now the snow would come and snow us in, but we would always go on marching. Legs, that would be everything now. For hours on end my gaze would be fixed on the wet earth. I would have time for remorse, for endless self-accusations. But I would always keep in step, swing my legs back and forth, and go on marching. Also, our marching would by now be more like a trot. Now and again, very far off, a mocking ridge of hills would appear, thin as the blade of a pocket knife, a sort of forest. And then we'd know that beyond this forest, whose edge we would reach after many hours, other endless plains extended. From time to time there would be shots. These scattered shots would remind us of what was coming, the battle which would one day have to be fought. And we would march. The officers would ride around with mournful expressions on their faces, adjutants would whip their horses past the column, as if they were being harried by fearful forebodings. One would think of the Emperor, the Commander-in-Chief, quite remotely, but, all the same, one would imagine him, and that would be consoling. And we would keep on marching. Countless small but terrible interruptions would hinder the march for short periods. Yet we would hardly notice them, but would go on marching. Then memories would come to me, not clear ones, and yet excessively clear ones. They would gobble at my heart like buzzards at a welcome prey, they would transport me to a cosy and homely place, to the golden, roundish vineyard hills wreathed with delicate mists. I would hear cowbells ringing and clamoring against my heart. A caressing sky would be curving with watery colors and full of sounds over my head. The ache would nearly madden me, but I would go on marching. My comrades to left and right, before and behind, that would be all that mattered. The legs would work like an old but still willing machine. Burning villages would be a daily sight for the eyes, no longer even interesting, and one would not be surprised by cruelties of an inhuman sort. Then one evening, in the ever-increasing bitter cold, my comrade, his name could be Tscharner, would drop to the ground. I would try to help him up, but the officer would give the command: "Let him lie there!" And we would go on marching. Then, one noon, we would see our Emperor, his face. But he would smile, he would enchant us. Yes, it wouldn't occur to this man to unnerve and discourage his soldiers by having a gloomy look on his face. Sure of victory, future battles won in advance, we would go on marching through the snow. And then, after endless marches, it would at last come to blows, and it is possible that I would remain alive and have gone on marching again. "Now we're off to Moscow, pal!" someone in our rank would say. I would decline to answer him, though I would not know why. I would be only a little cog in the machine of a great design, not a person any more. I would know nothing of parents any more, of relatives, songs, personal troubles or hopes, nothing of the meaning and magic of home any more. Soldierly discipline and patience would have made me into a firm and impenetrable, almost empty lump of body. And so the march would go on, toward Moscow. I wouldn't curse life, it would have long since become too abominable for cursing. I would feel no more pain, I would have finished with feeling pain and all its sudden tremors. That is roughly what it would be like, I think, as a soldier under Napoleon.

"You're a fine one," Kraus said to me, actually quite without reason, "you're one of those worthless fellows who think they're above the rules. I know. You needn't say anything. You think I'm a grumpy pedagogue and dogmatist. Well, I'm not. And what do you and your sort, big mouths, what do you suppose it really means to be serious and attentive? You imagine you're king, just because you can leap and dance around, definitely and quite rightfully, without a doubt, don't you? Oh, I can see through you, you dancer. Always laughing at what's right and proper, you can do that well enough, yes, yes, you're quite the master in that, you and your lot. But watch out, watch out. The storms and lightning and thunder and blows of fate certainly haven't yet been done away with, so as to save you the trouble. Just because of your gracefulness, you artists, for that's what you are, there certainly hasn't been any dropping-off in the difficulties facing anyone who really does something, who's really alive. Learn by heart the lesson in front of you, instead of trying to prove that you can look down on me and laugh. What a little gentleman! He wants to show me that he can act big if it happens to suit him. Let me tell you, Kraus simply despises such pitiful play-acting! Do something! That's the message for you, my lad, and telling you a dozen times over wouldn't stop you from turning up your noble nose. Do you know something, Jakob, lord of life: let me be. Go and make your conquests! I'm certain a few will fall at your feet, and they'll be there for the picking. Everything's soft on you, everything comes your way, you mop-maker. What? Still got your hands in your pockets? I see the point, yes. If the roast pigeons come flitting into a fellow's mouth, why ever should he take the trouble to look like someone who's ready for doing something, for work, for using his hands?

Yawn a little, won't you? That makes it easier. As things are, you're looking too self-possessed, controlled, and modest. Or do you want to read me a few rules? Go ahead. It would be very exciting. Oh, go away. Your silly presence confuses me, you old— I nearly said something there. Makes me say sinful things, gets my dander up, that's what he does. Make yourself invisible, or get busy with something. And you lose all your manners, yes, you do, when you're up before the Principal and the Fräulein. I've seen it. But what's the use of talking to a goof like you? Admit it, you'd be very nice if you weren't a fool. If you admit that, I'll hug you."
"O Kraus, dearest friend," I said, "are you, of all people, scoffing and jeering at me? Can Kraus do that? Is it possible?" I laughed aloud and sauntered to my room. Soon there'll be nothing here in the Benjamenta Institute but sauntering. It looks as if the "days are numbered" here. But people are wrong. Perhaps Fräulein Benjamenta is also wrong. Perhaps the Principal, too. Perhaps all of us are wrong.

I am a Croesus. The money, well, as for that— quiet, not a word about money. I'm leading a strange double life, a life that is regular and irregular, controlled and uncontrolled, simple and highly complicated. What does Herr Benjamenta mean when he says that he has never loved anyone? What does it mean when he says this to me, his pupil and slave? Yes, of course, pupils are slaves, young leaves, torn from branches and trunks, given up to the merciless gale, and already a little yellow as well. Is Herr Benjamenta a gale? It's quite conceivable, for I've often had occasion to feel the roarings and rages and dark explosions of this gale. And also he's so omnipotent, and I, a pupil, how tiny I am. Quiet now, not a word about omnipotence. One is always wrong when one takes up with big words. Herr Benjamenta is so prone to excitement and frailty, so very prone, that it almost makes me laugh, perhaps even grin. I think that everything, everything is frail, everything must needs tremble like worms. Yes, of course, and this illumination, this certainty, makes me a Croesus, that's to say, it makes me a Kraus. Kraus loves and hates nothing, therefore he is a Croesus, something in him verges on the inviolable. He's like a rock, and life, the stormy wave, breaks against his virtues. His nature, his character, is positively festooned with virtues. One can hardly love him, to hate him is unthinkable. One likes anything that is pretty and attractive, and that's why beauty and prettiness are so much exposed to being eaten up or abused. No consuming, guzzling fondnesses dare come anywhere near Kraus. How forsakenly he stands there, and yet how steadfastly, how unapproachably! Like a demigod. But nobody understands that, I don't either—sometimes I say and think things that surpass my own understanding. Perhaps, therefore, I should have been a parson, the founder of a religious sect or movement. Well, that could still happen. I can make anything of myself. But Benjamenta?— I'm certain that he'll soon tell me the story of his life. He's going to feel the urge to reveal things, to tell stories. Very probably. And oddly enough: sometimes I feel that I should never leave this man, this giant, never, as if we were fused into one. But one is always mistaken. I want to keep my self-possession, to some extent. Not too much, no. To be too self-possessed makes one cheeky. Why reckon on anything important in life? Must it be so? I'm so small. That's what I'll loosely hang on to, my smallness, smallness and worthlessness. And Fräulein Benjamenta? Will she really die? I daren't think of that, and I'm not allowed to, either. A higher sort of sentiment forbids me. No, I'm not a Croesus. And as for the double life, everybody lives one, actually. Why boast about it? Ah, all these thoughts, all this peculiar yearning, this seeking, this stretching out of hands toward a meaning. Let it all dream, let it all sleep. I'll simply let it come. Let it come.

I'm writing this in a hurry. I'm trembling all over. There are lights dancing and flickering before my eyes. Something terrible has happened, seems to have happened, I hardly know what it was. Herr Benjamenta has had a fit and tried to— strangle me. Is this true? I can't think straight, I can't say if what happened is true. But I'm so upset, it must be true. The Principal got so angry, it was indescribable. He was like a Samson, that man in the history of Palestine who shook the pillars of a tall house full of people till the festive, wanton palace, till the stone triumph, till naughtiness itself came tumbling down. Here, to be sure, that's to say less than an hour ago, there was nothing naughty, nothing vile, to be cast down, and there were also no pillars and columns, but it looked exactly the same, exactly, and I was frightened as never before, like a rabbit, terribly frightened. Yes, I was a rabbit, and indeed I had reason to run like a rabbit, I really would have been in trouble otherwise. I escaped with—I must say—marvelous agility from his throttling fists, and I think that I even bit Herr Benjamenta's, this Goliath's, finger. Perhaps that quick, energetic bite saved my life, for quite possibly the pain which the wound caused reminded him suddenly of good manners, reason, and humanity, so that conceivably I owe my life to a blatant offense against the rules of conduct for pupils. Certainly there was a danger of my being choked, but how did it all come about, how was it possible? He attacked me like a madman. He threw himself at me, his powerful body, like a dark lump of mad anger; it was coming at me like a wave, to batter me against hard sea walls. I'm inventing the water. That's nonsense, to be sure, but I'm still quite stunned, quite confused and shaken. "What are you doing, dear and honored Principal, hey?" I shrieked, and ran through the office door like a thing possessed. And there I listened again. As I stood, safe and sound, in the corridor, I put, trembling all over, of course, my ear to the keyhole, and listened. And I heard him quietly laughing in there. I ran all the way to the classroom table and here I am, and I don't know if I dreamed it or if it really did happen to me. No, no, it's real, it's a fact. If only Kraus would come! I'm still a bit scared. How nice it would be if dear Kraus would come and give me a scolding, as he often does, out of his Book of Commandments. I'd like to be scolded a little, told off, condemned and sentenced, that would do me no end of good. Am I childish?

I was never really a child, and therefore something in the nature of childhood will cling to me always, I'm certain. I have simply grown, become older, but my nature never changed. I enjoy mischief just as I did years ago, but that's just the point, actually I never played mischievous tricks. Once, very early on, I gave my brother a knock on the head. That just happened, it wasn't mischief. Certainly there was plenty of mischief and boyishness, but the idea always interested me more than the thing itself. I began, early on, to look for deep things everywhere, even in mischief. I don't develop. At least, that's what I claim. Perhaps I shall never put out twigs and branches. One day some fragrance or other will issue from my nature and my originating, I shall flower, and the fragrance will shed itself around a little, then I shall bow my head, which Kraus calls my stupid arrogant pig-head. My arms and legs will strangely sag, my mind, pride, and character, everything will crack and fade, and I shall be dead, not really dead, only dead in a certain sort of way, and then I shall vegetate and die for perhaps another sixty years. I shall grow old. But I'm not afraid of myself. I couldn't possibly inspire myself with dread. For I don't respect my ego at all, I merely see it, and it leaves me cold. Oh, to come in from the cold! How glorious! I shall be able to come into the warmth, over and over again, for nothing personal or selfish will ever stop me from becoming warm and catching fire and taking part. How fortunate I am, not to be able to see in myself anything worth respecting and watching! To be small and to stay small. And if a hand, a situation, a wave were ever to raise me up and carry me to where I could command power and influence, I would destroy the circumstances that had favored me, and I would hurl myself down into the humble, speechless, insignificant darkness. I can only breathe in the lower regions.

I quite agree with the rules which are—still—valid here, when they say that the eyes of the pupil and of the apprentice to life must shine with gaiety and good will. Yes, eyes must radiate steadfastness of soul. I despise tears, and yet I have been crying. More inwardly than outwardly, of course, but that is perhaps the most dreadful thing about it. Fräulein Benjamenta said to me: "Jakob, I am dying, because I have found no love. The heart which no deserving person deserved to possess and to wound, it is dying now. Adieu, Jakob, it's already time to say adieu. You boys, Kraus, you, and the others, you will sing a song by the bed in which I shall lie. You will mourn for me, softly. And each of you will lay a flower, perhaps still moist with nature's dew, upon my shroud. I want to take your young human heart into my sisterly and smiling confidence now. Yes, Jakob, to confide in you is so natural, for when you look as you are looking now, it's as if you must have ears, a hearing heart, and eyes, a soul, a compassionate understanding and fellow-feeling for everything and for each particular thing, even for what cannot be said and cannot be heard. I am dying of the incomprehension of those who could have seen me and held me, dying of the emptiness of cautious and clever people, and of the lovelessness of hesitancy and not-much-liking. Someone thought he would love me one day, thought he wanted to have me, but he hesitated, left me waiting, and I hesitated too, but then I'm a girl, I had to be hesitant, it was allowed and expected of me. Ah, how deceived I have been by disloyalty, tormented by the vacancy and unfeeling of a heart in which I believed, because I believed it was full of genuine and insistent feelings. If a thing can reflect and choose, it's not a feeling. I'm speaking to you of a man in whom my sweet and graceful dreams made me believe, believe without any hesitation. I can't tell you everything. I'd rather be silent. Oh, the annihilating thing that's killing me, Jakob! All the desolations that are crushing me!—but that's enough. Tell me, do you love me, as young brothers love their sisters? Good. Everything is good, just the way it is, don't you think, Jakob? We shan't grumble, shan't despair, the two of us, shall we? And it is beautiful, isn't it, not to want anything any more? Or isn't it? Yes, it is beautiful. Come, let me kiss you, just once, a kiss in innocence. Be soft. I know that you don't like to cry, but let's have a little cry together. And quietly now, quietly." She didn't say any more. It was as if she wanted to say many other things, but could find no more words for what she was feeling. Outside in the courtyard big wet snowflakes were falling. The inner chambers! And I had always thought of Fräulein Benjamenta as the mistress of these inner chambers. I have always thought of her as a tender princess. And now? Fräulein Benjamenta is suffering, tender, feminine person. Not a princess. So one day she will lie in there on the bed. Her mouth will be rigid, and around her lifeless brow the curls will be deceptively playing. But why picture this? I'm going to see the Principal now. He has sent for me. On one side of me the lament and the corpse of a girl, on the other side her brother, who seems never to have lived. Yes, Benjamenta seems to me like a starved and imprisoned tiger. And now? Now I'm going into his gaping jaws? Onward! I hope his courage will cool down at the sight of a defenseless pupil. I am at his disposal. I am afraid of him, but at the same time something in me laughs him to scorn. Moreover, he still owes me his life-story. He gave me a firm promise of it and I shall be sure to remind him. Yes, that is how he seems: he has never yet lived. Does he want to live through me now? Does he think living is fuller if you commit crimes? That would be stupid, very stupid, and dangerous. But I must! I must go to this man. Some soul-force that I don't understand is compelling me to go and listen to him, again and again, and to find out all about him. Let the Principal eat me if he wants to, in other words, let him do me any harm he likes. In any case I shall have perished in a big way. Now to the office. Poor Fräulein Benjamenta!—

A little scornfully, I must say, but otherwise very confidingly (yes, thus confidingly because scornfully), the Principal slapped me on the shoulder and laughed with his wide but well-shaped mouth. This made his teeth show. "Principal," I said, "I must ask you to treat me with somewhat less offensive friendliness. I am still your pupil. Moreover, I decline, and the word is not strong enough, your favors. You should be condescending and generous to such a menial fellow. My name is Jakob von Gunten, and he is a young person, but still conscious of his dignity. I am unforgivable, that I see, but also I am not to be humiliated, that I forbid." —And with these quite ridiculously arrogant words, with these words that were so little suited to the present age, I thrust away the Principal's hand. Then Herr Benjamenta laughed again, even more merrily, and said: "I have to contain myself, I can't help laughing at you, Jakob, and I shall kiss you if I'm not careful, you splendid boy." I exclaimed: "Kiss me? Are you mad, Principal? I hope not." I was myself amazed how easily I said that, and involuntarily I took a step backward, as if to avoid a blow. But Herr Benjamenta, all kindness and reticence, his lips trembling with strange gratification, said: "You, boy, are quite delectable. I would like to live with you in deserts or on icy mountains in the northern seas, it's most enticing. Come here! Ah, now, don't be afraid, please don't be afraid of me. I won't do anything to you. What could I do, whatever would I want to do to you? I can't help finding you estimable and rare, I do that, but it needn't frighten you. Besides, Jakob, and now in all seriousness, listen. Will you stay with me for keeps? You don't understand what I mean, really, so let me make it all quite plain. This place is finished, do you understand that?" I suddenly burst out with: "Ah, Principal, it's just as I suspected." He laughed and said: "Well, then, you suspected that the Benjamenta Institute is here today but will be gone tomorrow. Yes, that's for sure. You are the last pupil here. I'm not accepting any more. Look at me! I am so immensely pleased, you understand, that there was still time to get to know you, young Jakob, such a right sort of person, before I shut up shop forever. And now I'm asking you, you scamp, who have bound me with such peculiar and happy chains, will you go along with me, shall we stay together, start something together, do and dare and achieve something, shall we both, you the little one and I the big one, try to stand up to life together? Please answer me at once." I replied: "In my view, my answer to this question needs time, Principal. But what you say interests me, and I shall think over the matter between now and tomorrow. But I think my answer will be yes." Herr Benjamenta, it seemed, could hardly restrain himself, and he said: "You are enchanting." After a pause, he began again: "For look, together with you one could survive something like danger, like a daring and adventurous voyage of discovery. But we could also easily do something refined and polite. You have both kinds of blood: gentle and fearless. Together with you, one can venture either something courageous or something very delicate." "Principal," I said, "don't flatter me, that is horrid and suspicious. And stop! Where is the story of your life, which you promised to tell me, as you will surely remember?" At this moment somebody tore open the door. Kraus, it was he, rushed breathless and pale, and unable to deliver the message which he had, obviously, on his lips, into the room. He only made a rapid gesture, telling us to come. We all three went into the darkening classroom. What we saw here froze us in our tracks.

On the floor lay the lifeless Fräulein. The Principal took her hand, but let it go again, as if a snake had bitten him, and moved back, shuddering with horror. Then he returned to the dead girl, looked at her, went away again, only to return once more. Kraus was kneeling at her feet. I was holding the instructress's head in both hands, so that it would not need to touch the hard floor. Her eyes were still open, not very wide, but as if she were smiling. Herr Benjamenta closed them. He, too, was kneeling on the floor. None of us said anything, and we weren't "plunged in thought." I, at least, could think of nothing definite at all. But I was quite calm. I even felt, vain as it may sound, good and beautiful. From somewhere I heard a very thin trickling of melody. Lines and rays were moving and crisscrossing before my eyes. "Take hold of her," said the Principal quietly, "come! Carry her into the livingroom. Take her gently, oh, gently. Careful, Kraus. For God's sake, not so rough. Jakob, be careful now, will you? Don't knock her against anything. I'll help you. Forward now, very slowly. That's right. And someone reach out and open the door. That's it, that's it. We can do it. Only careful now." His words were unnecessary, in my opinion. We carried Fräulein Benjamenta to the bed, the Principal quickly pulling away the cover, and now she lay there, just as she had told me she would, in advance, as it were. And then the pupils came in and they all saw it, and then we all stood there, by the bed. The Principal gave us a sign, which we understood, and we pupils and boys began to sing softly in chorus. It was the lament which the girl had wanted to hear when she lay on the bed. And now, so I imagined, she heard the quiet song. I think we all felt as if it were a class and we were singing as the instructress told us to, whose commands we were always so quick to obey. When we had finished the song, Kraus stepped from the semicircle we had formed and spoke as follows, a little slowly, but giving all the more weight to his words: "Sleep, rest sweetly, dear and honored Fräulein. Thou art free from the difficulties, from the fears, from the troubles and events of life. (He addressed her as "Thou." I liked that.) We have sung at thy bedside, as thou hast commanded. Are we, thy pupils, now all forsaken? That is how it seems, and it is so. Yet thou who hast died before thy time, will never disappear, never, from our memories. Thou shalt remain alive in our hearts. We, thy boys, whom thou has commanded and ruled, we shall be scattered abroad into rest-less and wearisome life, seeking gain and seeking a home, and perhaps we shall never find and see one another again. But we shall all think of thee, our instructress, because the thoughts which thou has planted in our minds, the teachings and knowledge which thou hast secured in us, will always remind us of thee, creator of goodness. Quite of their own accord. When we eat, the fork will tell us how thou has desired us to handle and manage it, and we shall sit decently at table, and the knowledge that we are doing so will make us think of thee. In us, thy guidance, thy com-mands, thy life, thy teachings, thy questions, and thy voice's sound shall continue. If one of us pupils gets further in life than the others, he will perhaps no longer wish to know those whom he has left behind, if ever they should meet again. Certainly. But then he will be sure to remember the Benjamenta Institute and its lady, and he will be ashamed to have so quickly and arrogantly denied and forgotten thy precepts. Then without hesitation he will stretch out his hand in greeting to his friend, his brother, this other person. What were thy teachings, O dear departed one? Thou hast always told us that we should be modest and willing. Ah, we shall never forget this, as little as we shall be able to surpass and forget the dear person who told us this. Sleep well! Dream! Lovely imagin-ings may be floating and whispering around thee. May Loyalty, who is near to thee, bow to thee its knee, and Graceful Devotion and Memory, wanton with unending tender remembrances, scatter blossoms, branches, flowers, and words of love around thy brow and hands. We, thy pupils, would like now to sing one more song, and then we shall be certain that we have prayed at thy deathbed, which will be for us a bed of joy, of happy and devoted memory. For thou hast taught us to pray. Thou hast said: Singing is praying. And thou shalt hear us, and we shall imagine that thou art smiling. It is such grief for our hearts to see thee lying here, for thy movements were to us as refreshing spring-water to a man who thirsts. Yes, it is a grievous sorrow. But we are masters of ourselves, and certainly thou wouldst have wished for that as well. Thus we are tranquil. Thus we obey thee and sing." Kraus stepped back from the bed and we sang another song, with sounds coming and going as softly as those of the first. Then we walked, in turn, to the bed, and each of us pressed a kiss on the hand of the dead girl. And each of us pupils said something. Hans said: "I shall tell Schilinski. And Heinrich must be told, too." Schacht said: "Goodbye, thou wast always so kind." Peter said: "I shall do thy commands." Then we went back to the classroom, leaving the brother alone with the sister, the Principal with the Principaless, the living man with the dead girl, the lonely man with the lonely girl, the man bowed by sorrows, Herr Benjamenta, alone with Fräulein Benjamenta, blessèd, dead and gone.

I have had to say goodbye to Kraus. Kraus has gone. A light, a sun, has disappeared. I feel that from now on it could only be evening in the world and all around me. Before a sun sets, it casts reddish rays across the darkening present, so did Kraus. Before he went, he gave me one more quick scolding, and as he did so the whole veritable Kraus was radiantly manifest for the last time. "Adieu, Jakob, improve yourself, change yourself," he said to me as he held out his hand, almost annoyed at having to do so. "I'm going now, out into the world, into service. I hope you will have to do this soon too. It certainly won't do you any harm. I hope your incomprehension gets a few hard knocks. Someone ought to take you by your naughty ears. Don't laugh now that

we're saying goodbye. Though it suits you. And who knows, perhaps things in this world are so foolish that they'll haul you up to
the heights. Then you can quietly and cheekily carry on with your
shameless ways, your defiance, your arrogance and smiling indolence, with your mockery and all kinds of mischief, and keep yourself carefree, as you are. Then you'll be able to boast until you burst
about all the bad habits that they haven't been able to rid you of
here in the Benjamenta Institute. But I hope that worry and toil
will take you into their hard, vice-breaking school. Look, Kraus is
saying hard words. But perhaps I mean it better for you, Brother
Funny, than people who would wish you good luck to your gaping
face. Work more, wish less, and something else: please forget all
about me. I would only be annoyed if I felt that you might have
one of your shabby old cast-off, dancing, here-today-and-gone-
tomorrow thoughts left over for me. No, pal, realize this, Kraus
doesn't need any of your von Guntenish jokes." "You dear, loveless
friend," I exclaimed, full of frightened farewell thoughts and feelings. And I wanted to hug him. But he stopped that in the simplest
way in the world, just by quickly going, and forever. "The Benjamenta Institute is here today and will be gone tomorrow," I
said to myself. I went to see the Principal. I felt as if the world
had been rent apart by a glowing, fiery, yawning gulf between one
spatial possibility and the diametrically opposite one. With Kraus,
the half of life was gone. "From now on, a different life!" I mur-
mured. Besides, it's quite simple: I was sad and a little stunned.
Why go off into big words? To the Principal I bowed more cere-
moniously than ever, and it seemed appropriate to say: "Good
day, Principal." "Are you mad, my boy?" he shouted. He came toward me and would have embraced me, but I stopped him with a
knock on his outstretched arm. "Kraus has gone," I said, very

gravely. We were silent and contented ourselves with looking at one another for a fairly long time.

Then Herr Benjamenta said in a quiet manly voice: "I have found jobs today for all the others, your comrades. Now only we three are left here, you, me, and her lying on the bed. She (why not talk of the dead? They're alive, aren't they?) will be taken away tomorrow. That's an ugly thought, but a necessary one. And we shall sit up all night. We two shall have a talk by her bedside. And when I think how one day you arrived with your request, demand, and question, wanting to be admitted to the school, I'm seized by a terrific zest for life and for laughter. I'm over forty years old. Is that old? It was, but now that you're here, Jakob, it means youth, all green and budding, this being forty. With you, you heart of a boy, fresh life, life itself for the first time, came over me and into me. Here in this office, you see, I was desperate, I was drying up, I had positively buried myself. I hated the world, hated it, hated it. All this being and moving and living, I hated it unspeakably and avoided it. Then you came in, fresh, silly, impolite, cheeky, and blossoming, fragrant with unspoilt feelings, and quite naturally I gave you a mighty ticking-off, but I knew, the moment I saw you, that you were a magnificent fellow, flown down, I felt, from heaven for me, sent to me and given to me by an all-knowing God. Yes, it was you I needed, and I always smiled secretly when you came in from time to time, to pester me with your delightful cheek and clumsiness, which looked to me like successful works of art. Oh, no, not to pester, but to infatuate me. Stop it, Benjamenta, stop it. —Tell me, didn't you ever notice that we two were friends? Don't say anything. And when I kept my dignity, I would have liked to tear it to shreds. And even today that bow you gave was quite insanely ceremonious! But listen, how about my attack of rage recently? Did I want to hurt you? Did I want to play a deadly trick on myself? Perhaps you know, Jakob? Yes? Then tell me, please, at once. At once, do you understand? What's happening to me? What is it? What do you say?" "I don't know, I thought you were mad, Principal," I said. Cold shudders ran through me as I saw the tenderness and zest for life showing all over his face. We said nothing for a while. Suddenly it occurred to me to remind Herr Benjamenta about the story of his life. That was very good. That might distract him, restrain him from fresh murderous attacks. I was at this moment firmly convinced that I was in the clutches of a semi-lunatic, and so I quickly said, with the sweat running down my forehead: "Yes, your life story, Principal, how about it? Do you know that I don't like hints? You gave me a dark hint that you were a dethroned ruler. Now then. Please express yourself clearly. I'm very much looking forward to it." He scratched behind his ear, quite embarrassed. Then suddenly he became really angry, pettily angry, and he shouted at me with a sergeant's voice: "Dismissed! Leave me alone!" Well, I didn't need telling twice, but vanished immediately. Was he ashamed, was he tormented by something, this King Benjamenta, this lion in his cage? Anyway I was very glad to be able to stand outside in the corridor and listen. It was deathly quiet in there. I went to my room, lit the stump of a candle, and sat gazing at the picture of Mamma, which I had always carefully kept. Later, there was a knock at the door. It was the Principal, he was dressed all in black. "Come," he ordered, with iron severity. We went into the livingroom, to keep vigil by the body of Fräulein Benjamenta. Herr Benjamenta showed me, with gestures, to my seat. We sat down. Thank heavens, at least I didn't feel at all tired. I was very glad of that. The dead girl's face was still beautiful, yes, it even seemed to have become more graceful, and another thing: as the moments passed more and more beauty, feeling, and grace seemed to descend upon it. Something like a smiling forgiveness for mistakes of every kind seemed to float around and echo softly around the room. There was a sort of chirping. And it was so light, a bright seriousness in the room. Nothing dismal, nothing at all. I had a good feeling, because simply to be watching made me feel the pleasant peace that comes from quietly doing what it is one's duty to do.

"Later, Jakob," the Principal started to say, as we sat there, "later I'll tell you everything. For we shall stay together. I am certain, quite certain, that you'll agree to do this. Tomorrow, when I ask you for your decision, you won't say no, I'm certain. For today, I must tell you that I'm not really a dethroned king, I only put it that way for the sake of the image. Of course, there were times when this Benjamenta, who is sitting beside you, felt himself a lord, a conqueror, a king, when life lay before me to be seized on, when I believed with all my senses in the future and in greatness, when my footsteps carried me elastically along as over carpet-like meadows and encouragements, when I possessed all I saw, enjoyed everything I fleetingly thought of, when everything was ready to crown me with satisfaction, to anoint me with successes and achievements, when I was king without really noticing it, great without needing consciously to take account of it. In this sense, Jakob, I have been exalted, that's to say, simply young and promising, and in this sense the deposing and dethronement also occurred. I collapsed.

And I doubted myself and everything. When one despairs and is sad, dear Jakob, one is so miserably small, and more and more small things hurl themselves over one, like greedy, fast-moving vermin eating us, very slowly, managing to choke us, to unman us, very slowly. But that bit about the king was just a figure of speech. I apologize, little listener, if I made you believe in a scepter and purple robes. But I think you really knew what was meant by these kingdoms in stammerings and sighs. I seem a bit more cosy to you now, don't I? Now that I'm not a king? For even you will admit that rulers who are compelled to give lessons, et cetera, and to found institutes, must certainly be pretty dismal characters. No, no, I was proud and happy only for the future: those were my estates and royal revenues. Then for long years I was discouraged and humiliated. And now I am again, that is, I am beginning again, to be myself, and I feel as if I had inherited a fortune, good heavens no, not that, no, I feel as if I—had been raised up and crowned ruler. Of course the dark moments, the cruelly dark moments still come, when there's blackness all around me and around my burnt and charred heart, as it were, don't misunderstand me, everything is detestable, and at such moments I have an urge to destroy, to kill. O my soul, you, would you stay with me still, now that you know this? Could you, perhaps out of a simple liking for me, or out of any other feeling that appeals to you, decide to defy the danger of being together with a monster like me? Can you be defiant with a high heart? Are you that sort of a defiant person? And will you or won't you hold all this against me? Against me? Ah, how silly. Besides, Jakob, I know that we shall live together. It is decided. Why still question you? Look, I do know my former pupil. You aren't my pupil any more now, Jakob. I don't want to educate and teach you any more, I want to live and, living, to shoulder some burden, carry it, and do something. Oh, it would be glorious, so glorious, to suffer with such a heart for one's friend. I have what I wanted to have and so I feel as if I could do everything, could endure and gladly suffer everything. No more thoughts, no more words. Please don't say anything. Tell me tomorrow, after this life there on the bed has been carried away, after I've been able to shed the purely external ceremony and turn it into an inward one, then tell me your opinion. You'll say yes, or you'll say no. Realize, you're completely free now. You can say or do whatever you like." Very quietly I said, trembling with a desire to give this all too confident person a bit of a fright: "But how shall I eat, Principal? You get homes for the others, and not for me? I find that strange. It isn't right. And I insist on it. It's your duty to find me a decent job. All I want is a job." Ah, he shuddered. He jumped. How I giggled, inside. Devilment is the nicest thing in life. Herr Benjamenta said sadly: "You're right. The correct thing is to get you a position, on the basis of your leaving-certificate. Certainly, you're quite right. Only I thought, only—I thought—that you might make an exception." I exclaimed in a blaze of dismay: "Exception? I make no exceptions. That is not fitting for the son of an alderman. My modesty, my birth, all my feelings forbid me to wish for more than what my fellow-pupils have received." From then on, he spoke not another word. I liked leaving Herr Benjamenta in a state of visible, and for me flattering, uncertainty. We spent the rest of the night in silence.

But sleep did overcome me as I sat there at our vigil. Not for long, for half an hour, or perhaps a little longer, I was rapt away from reality. I dreamed (the dream, I remember, shot down upon me from above, violently, showering me with rays of light) that I was in a meadow on a mountainside. It was a dark, velvety green. And it was embroidered all over with flowers, like kisses in the shapes of flowers. It was nature, and yet not so, image and body at the same time. A wonderfully beautiful girl lay on the meadow, I told myself it must be the instructress, but quickly I said: "No, it can't be. We haven't got an instructress any more." Well, then, it must have been some-body else, and I positively saw how I was consoling myself, and I heard the consoling. It said: "Bah! Stop all this interpreting!" The girl was naked, undulant and shining. On one of her beau-tiful legs there was a garter, softly fluttering in the wind that was caressing everything. It seemed as if the whole dream was flutter-ing, the whole sweet dream, clear as a mirror. How happy I was! For a fleeting moment I thought of "This Person." Naturally it was the Principal of whom I was thinking. Suddenly I saw him, mounted on a high horse and clad in a shimmering, black, noble, and serious suit of armor. The long sword hung down at his side and the horse whinnied pugnaciously. "Well, just look now. There's the Principal on horseback," I thought, and I shouted, as loud as I could, so that the echoes rang in the gorges and ravines: "I have made my decision." But he didn't hear me. Agonized, I shouted: "Hey! Principal! Listen!" But no, he turned his back on me. He was looking into the distance, out and down into life. And he didn't even turn his head. For my benefit, it seems, the dream now rolled on, bit by bit, like a wagon, and then we found ourselves, I and "This Person," naturally no other than Herr Benjamenta, in the middle of the desert. We were travel-ing and doing business with the desert dwellers, and we were quite peculiarly animated by a cool, I might say splendid, contentment. It looked as if we had both escaped forever, or at least for a very long time, from what people call European culture. "Aha," I thought, involuntarily, and, it seemed to me, rather foolishly, "so that was it, that was it!" But what it was, the thing I thought, I couldn't puzzle out. We wandered on. Then a throng of hostile people appeared, but we dispersed them, though I really don't know how it happened. The regions of the earth shot like lightning past us on our days of wandering. I knew the experience of entire long decades of tribulation, signaling as they passed us by. How peculiar that was. The particular weeks eyed one another like small, glittering gems. It was ridiculous and it was glorious too. "Getting away from culture, Jakob, you know, it's wonderful," said the Principal from time to time, looking like an Arab. We were riding camels. And the customs of the people we saw delighted us. There was something mysterious, gentle, and delicate in the movements of these countries. Yes, it was as if they were marching along, no, flying along. The sea extended majestically like a great blue wet world of thought. One moment I heard the wingbeats of birds, then animals bellowing, then trees rustling overhead. "So you did come along, then. I knew you would," said Herr Benjamenta, whom the Indians had made a Prince. How crazy! As cruelly exciting as it may sound: the fact was, we were organizing a revolution in India. And apparently the trick worked. It was delicious to be alive, I felt it in every limb. Life was flourishing before our far-seeing gaze, like a tree with branches and twigs. And how steadfast we were! And through dangers and experiences we waded as through icy waters that were a balm to our heat. I was always the Squire and the Principal was the Knight. "Well and good," I suddenly thought. And as I was thinking this, I woke up and looked around in the livingroom. Herr Benjamenta had fallen asleep too. I woke him up by telling him: "How can you sleep, Principal! But permit me to tell you that I've decided to go with you, wherever you want to go." We shook hands, and that meant a great deal.

I'm packing. Yes, we two, the Principal and I, we are busy packing, really packing everything up, leaving, clearing out, tearing things apart, pushing and shoving. We shall travel. Well and good. This person suits me and I'm not asking myself why any more. I feel that life demands impulses, not considerations. Today I shall say adieu to my brother. I shall leave nothing here. Nothing's keeping me, nothing obliges me to say: "How would it be if . . ." No, there's nothing left to be woulding and iffing about. Fräulein Benjamenta is under the ground. The pupils, my friends, are scattered in all kinds of jobs. And if I am smashed to pieces and go to ruin, what is being smashed and ruined? A zero. The individual me is only a zero. But now I'll throw away my pen! Away with the life of thought! I'm going with Herr Benjamenta into the desert. I just want to see if one can live and breathe and be in the wilderness too, willing good things and doing them, and sleeping and dreaming at night. What's all this. I don't want to think of anything more now. Not even of God? No! God will be with me. What should I need to think of Him? God goes with thoughtless people. So now adieu, Benjamenta Institute.